ROUMELIA LANE

stormy encounter

HARLEQUIN BOOKS
toronto-winnipeg

© Roumelia Lane 1974

Original hard cover edition published in 1974
by Mills & Boon Limited

SBN 373-70591-3
Harlequin Presents edition published May 1975

Printed in Canada.

CHAPTER ONE

THE March winds had finally blown themselves out, and the beech trees lining the square stretched themselves tentatively in the pale April dawn.

The whine of an electrically powered milk cart broke the sleepy silence, cutting into it delicately as it came round the corner, then rattling over the cobblestones energetically as though to give an extra prod to those tucked up in their beds who might be tempted to ignore it.

Janet allowed herself enough time to pull the curtains back on the scene and muse over what to wear, then she scurried round to get ready for work.

In the cluttered bathroom, with nylons and smalls strung across a line near the immersion heater, and sheets and towels overflowing in the linen basket, waiting for the launderette, she washed and dressed from the bundle of clothes she had brought in with her—tweed-speckled suit, leaf-green blouse, stockings, and glossy medium-heeled shoes.

At the mirror she applied a speedy touch of make-up. With her red-brown hair swept back from her forehead to fall in a soft wave on either side of her face, wide-set golden-brown eyes and a sparkling smile, she knew she was attractive, but she had no time to gloat over it. With her living to earn and half the rent of the flat to find each week she was fully occupied with the business of making enough money to fill her needs.

Of course her job with the secretarial agency paid well, but after everything had been carefully budgeted for, with very little to spare, it didn't allow for much slacking on her part.

She dropped her comb into her handbag after applying the finishing touches to her hair and went along to the kitchen. On her way there she ran into a sleepy dishevelled figure stumbling towards the bathroom. From the midst of towel, toilet bag, and bright yellow curlers, she heard a mumbled, 'Sorry, old girl. I didn't hear the alarm.'

Janet smiled after her flatmate. 'Don't worry, I'll put the kettle on,' she said comfortingly.

Nona, with dark hair and dark-fringed serious blue eyes, was twenty-two, the same age as herself. They had known each other from schooldays, and had gravitated to London together. There had been five of them at first and they had taken a big flat over in Clapham, but with half the girls not taking their share in the chores, and general dissatisfaction reigning for most of the time, the five had gradually split up.

Janet and Nona had moved into this flat in Fulham. They found they got on well together, neither one being content to sit back and let the other do all the work.

The flat was nothing fabulous, if anything it was rather shabby, but they had their own front door, and it was handy for the buses and tubes. It consisted of a long hall leading from a flight of stone steps outside, with two small rooms used as bedrooms, plus a bathroom at the end, on one side, and a kitchen and a living room on the other side.

From the bathroom now came the sound of tuneful humming as Nona gradually woke up to the day. Filling the kettle and lighting the gas stove, Janet mused good-naturedly on her friend's elated spirits these days. She hadn't missed the dreamy look in Nona's eyes over the past few weeks, and she knew she was keeping company with one of the young managers at the store where she worked.

Though Janet envied her starry-eyed look, she wasn't greatly put out by the lack of romance in her own life. She had been on the occasional date, and gone to the usual parties, but as yet she had met no man who had made an earth-

6

shattering impact on her. Nor was she in any great hurry to.

It was true she had to work hard to support herself in London, but she did it from choice. She had two sisters married and living in the same town on the Suffolk coast, and a brother and his family settled in Cambridge. With her widowed mother living abroad she would have been welcomed by any one of them to stay as long as she wished. However, she liked the independence of looking after herself and at least there was always plenty of work in London.

She set out cups and saucers and plates, and while she was waiting for the kettle to boil she went out along the hall to the letterbox behind the front door.

There were the usual bills. The quarterly demand for the telephone. The reminder that the gas payment was due, and the milkman's bill which he had dropped in through the letterbox. Flicking through this depressing lot, Janet found a bright spot in the picturesque Spanish stamp and an envelope addressed in her mother's sprawling handwriting. There was also a letter for Nona from her brother who was serving with the Air Force in Canada.

With the sheaf of mail in her hand, her mother's letter uppermost, Janet opened the door to pick up the bottle of milk standing outside. She didn't feel the cold blast of air on her cheek, nor did she see the row of sombre dark houses opposite, the windows of the other early risers lit here and there in the semi-light of early morning. In her mind's eye she saw vivid blue skies and a small white house pulsing in the heat of Ibiza.

Her mother, loving the sun, and with nothing to keep her in England, had yearned to make the island her permanent home. The whole family had encouraged her and when she had found the house she could afford out of what their father had managed to provide for her before he died, Janet and Nona had gone out the summer before last to help her to settle in.

But for an adjoining villa which was closed up most of the time, she lived in the heart of the countryside. She managed on a slender income, but she was supremely happy, and as she had a telephone on which she could get in direct contact with the flat, Janet was content. The memory of that fortnight's holiday of two years ago always fresh in her mind, she loved to hear about the island in her mother's letters.

The kettle was boiling when she got back to the kitchen. She made the tea, and dropped four slices of bread in the toaster, buttering it hot when it popped up. Nona came into the kitchen and poured the tea, and cut the toast. Then when they were settled she pounced on her brother's letter, reading it avidly as she munched.

Janet smiled on her indulgently. The young man whose photograph stood on the old-fashioned sideboard in the front room was all the family Nona had. She knew brother and sister were very close.

She didn't open her mother's letter beside her plate. She preferred to anticipate its contents and read it later at her leisure. It was only when she had finished breakfast, and found that she had a good ten minutes to spare, that she decided to have a quick peep.

Nona had consumed the contents of her own letter greedily and was re-folding it, exclaiming happily, 'Oh, good! Peter says he thinks he'll be back in England by May.'

'Lovely,' Janet smiled absently, her eyes caught by her mother's large scrawly writing.

Her smile lingered as she started to read. Then gradually it became set. On the second page it disappeared, leaving the full soft lips tightened in a thin line. At the end of the letter her mouth was clamped solidly over a rising anger. 'Well, what a nerve!' The words burst out hotly as her brown eyes grew stormy.

'What's wrong?' Nona asked, taking a gulp of tea and keeping one eye on the clock

'The villa next to Mother's has been sold,' Janet explained gloweringly. 'The new people are a rich socialising couple who seem to be entertaining half the island.'

Nona looked sympathetic. 'Poor Mrs Kendall. Is it very noisy?' she asked.

'It's not that.' Janet drooped a lame smile over the letter. 'Being Mother she likes a bit of action. And isn't it just like her,' she tapped the scrawled pages with affectionate exasperation, 'to mention only in passing the worst part about the disused railway track!'

'The old track? You mean the length that runs up past the front of her house?' Nona's blue eyes widened with suspense.

'That's right, and alongside the villa,' Janet nodded. 'Well apparently, just lately it's been overrun with cars, and the villa people have said they intend to make it their own.'

'What!' Nona sat up. 'Well, they can't do that, can they? I mean, isn't it your mother's only entrance?'

'It is. And I know for a fact that she was told when she bought the house that the strip of track would be hers for a few hundred pesetas as soon as the legal details were sorted out.'

'Wasn't that some time ago?' Nona pointed out dubiously.

'Two years. But nothing moves with any great haste over there,' Janet shrugged. 'Apart from the odd farm cart going by along the track now and again, no one has bothered, and Mother has always considered the strip as her own drive.'

Nona looked concerned. 'Can these new people step in and buy it over her head, do you think?' she asked.

'If money's anything to do with it, they can,' Janet fumed. 'And as they have a perfectly good entrance on the road at the front, it would be downright unfair.'

'But surely, if your mother was there first, she should have first claim to it?' Nona offered.

'You would think so, wouldn't you?' Janet said wryly, a

bitter light in her brown eyes. Her glance strayed to the clock and she jumped up. 'Heavens, look at the time! I'll miss my bus!'

She grabbed up her coat and handbag and stuffing her mother's letter in her pocket she dashed for the door to the cheerful cries from Nona, who having another ten minutes to spare was rinsing off the breakfast crockery, 'Run girl! You'll catch it.'

Breathless and on the crowded bus, Janet entered into the whirl of the working day. Throughout it the contents of her mother's letter stayed with her to rankle. After a morning's typing, she ate her lunch in a modest restaurant, over a lump of resentment in her chest. It was the injustice of it that galled her.

On her way home across the city in the evening, in the blustering rain, she nursed her vexation behind set features, oblivious to the crush and push of people around her.

She was always the first to arrive back at the flat. By the time Nona's footsteps sounded on the steps outside she had the gas fire burning cheerily in the living room and a tray with coffee and biscuits all ready.

Nona fell in on a gust of wind and rain and a breathless, 'Phew, it's pouring, and I didn't take my brolly.'

'Get your wet things off and come and have some hot coffee,' Janet said from the front room. 'I've got the potatoes on.'

'Oh, good! And I've got the steak and a tin of peas.' Nona disrobed on her way to her bedroom across the hall. Discarding wet stockings and shoes for slacks and slippers, and pulling into a comfortable woolly, she chatted on, 'The apples looked rather nice, so I bought a couple for afters.'

'Lovely.' Janet smiled across to her, though there was a certain gravity in her brown eyes.

Not slow to sense a mood, Nona scuffed in and took her small stool beside the fire. When Janet was settled and they were sipping steaming coffee companionably and munching on sweet biscuits, Nona said practically, 'Well, come on, out with it. You've got something on your mind, I can tell.'

Janet placed her cup down and grimaced lightly. 'Is it that obvious?' She pulled in a deep breath as though wondering where to start. Then with a straight look at her friend she said purposefully, 'I'm going out to Ibiza.'

Nona's face showed no surprise. 'Because of that letter you got this morning?' She nodded.

Incensed at the thought of it, Janet explained with quiet fury, 'I can't sit back and let these people walk over Mother.'

'Of course you can't. If it was me I should want to do exactly the same,' said Nona.

Janet looked at her friend. Then she breathed a grateful sigh. 'I guessed you'd understand, Nona, but it's a relief to know you don't mind.' She drew a slip of paper towards her which had been lying beside the coffee pot. 'I've put everything down that you'll need for my half share of the bills. Trouble is...' she bit on her lower lip, 'I shan't feel right in coming back until I know that Mother is going to get what belongs to her, and that creates the problem of keeping up the rent of the flat.'

'It shouldn't affect us,' Nona said helpfully. 'Angela will be up here by the end of next week.'

Janet brightened. 'Is it as soon as that?' she said reflectively.

Their mutual friend was coming up to London to do a summer modelling assignment for her firm. She had tried frantically to get somewhere to live within reasonable distance of her work without success, and in the end Janet and Nona had offered to take her in with them.

'I don't know how we expected to put her up with only two beds,' Nona said humorously. 'Anyway, now she'll be able to use your room, and she's always insisted on paying half the rent.'

'That's right.' Janet nodded, relaxing gradually as one by

11

one the domestic cares fell away from her. She went on trailing her pencil down the figures on the list and watching it Nona asked, her practical side asserting itself, 'There's just one thing. What are you going to use for money? The air fare to Ibiza will cost a bit, won't it?'

Janet looked up and frowned apologetically at her flat-mate. 'That's the worst part of it, I'm afraid,' she sighed. 'I'm going to have to dig in quite deep to my holiday savings, and unless a miracle happens when I get back, I don't see how I'm going to afford to go on our trip to Greece.'

'Don't worry about it!' Nona urged her out of her despondency and patted her shoulder reassuringly. 'I know several girls at work who would be willing to take your place. Besides . . .' the dreamy look came into her eyes, 'I'm not certain to go myself yet . . .'

Silence descended while each girl followed the line of their own thoughts. Then above the hiss of the gas fire Nona asked,

'Have you told your mother you're going over?'

'No.' Janet got up and gathered together the coffee cups on the tray. 'I'm waiting until after seven o'clock. The telephone rate will be cheaper then.'

When the evening dinner dishes had been washed and replaced on their shelves, and the cooking odours had dispersed along the alley that the kitchen window opened on to, Janet went along the hall to the phone on the wall.

It never ceased to be a source of wonder to her that, since the laying of the new cables off the Spanish coast, she was able to ring her mother direct in her Ibizan cottage.

She dialled her number and almost before she had time to flick her glance over the old-fashioned barometer on the wall, the signal that she was through came in the soft whir-ring tones. In a moment that familiar sprightly voice was on the line.

'Mother, this is Janet,' she said, wasting no time. 'I'm just making a quick call.'

'Why, dear, how nice!' Mrs Kendall's voice was high-pitched with delight. 'Did you get my letter?'

'I did. And I think it's scandalous the way these villa people are trying to take your drive away from you.' Before her mother could take up precious time prattling over the subject, she went on, 'That's why I'm ringing. I'm coming out there.'

'But, dear,' Mrs Kendall chirped dubiously, 'do you have to? I mean ... well, what can we do?'

'We'll talk about that when I get there,' Janet said, partly to save time and expense on the phone, and partly because she really didn't know yet herself. But it seemed to her that, as all the rest of the family had domestic ties, and as her mother had no one to stand up for her, it was up to her as the unattached daughter to go out there and see that no one took advantage of a defenceless widow. 'Now don't worry about my arrival,' she said soothingly. 'I'll get a taxi from the airport. There should be a plane seat available tomorrow, and I'll probably land late afternoon or early evening.'

'All right, Jan dear,' Mrs Kendall agreed obediently. She managed to sing in gaily over the line in between their quick goodbyes and ringing off, 'It will be wonderful seeing you!'

Janet boarded the airport coach the next afternoon with a certain feeling of accomplishment. She had packed two suitcases the night before and spent this morning getting leave from her job, going to the bank, and settling up with Nona in the form of an envelope with money in it, placed under the clock in the kitchen. Taking a tube, with her luggage, to the West End, she had been able to book a seat on a plane to Ibiza with a travel agency. As the holiday season wasn't yet under way there were only two direct flights a week. Luckily one of them left that afternoon at three o'clock.

13

The coach was quite full. She took her seat amongst obviously wealthy sun-seekers, with a certain flutter of excitement. It would have been nice if she had been going out to her mother under rather less grim circumstances.

Reminding herself that she wasn't, she spent the whole journey to the airport fuming over the cheek of some people. Imagine—trying to browbeat her mother like that!

When they arrived where the thunder of plane engines rent the air and the cold wind swept across the runways she struggled with her two suitcases to the weigh-in, in reception, completely immersed in her stormy reverie of the island's social set.

Oh, she knew the type all right! Just because they were wealthy they thought it gave them the right to throw their weight about. Well, they would soon learn different when *she* arrived. She didn't intend to be overawed by any one of them.

While she waited in the queue at the weigh-in, her gaze came to rest with animosity on an expensive set of luggage belonging to a man who was standing off to one side. Putting her thoughts into practice, she fixed him with a haughty look, making no attempt to move her gaze until she was ready. He gave her a wintry blue stare, turning as an airport official came hurrying up, accompanied by two porters. She watched cynically as the porters took care of his expensive bags, and he was led smilingly away.

Her turn came to hump up her suitcases on to the scales. She saw with relief that what she had packed came within the weight allowed. She left the attendant thumping on sticky labels and went off to the lounge to await the time of her flight.

Quite a few people rushed for the appropriate door when the announcement finally came over the loudspeakers. Unprepared, her head in a magazine, Janet found herself almost at the end of the queue out to the bus that would take them to the plane. She was jammed in as one of the last and felt the sliding doors swish to only inches from her nose.

This uncomfortable state of affairs turned out to be quite an advantage, however, when they arrived where the screaming engines of the jet mingled with the wind gusting over the tarmac. Being one of the last on, she was one of the first off. She wasted no time in answering the welcoming smile of the stewardess who was beckoning her towards the boarding steps at the rear of the jet.

She hurried up out of the wind and met more of the smiling plane staff as she moved, a little excitedly, down the aisle between the seats. She had only flown once before, and as she had the whole plane to herself to start with, it seemed to her that it would be rather fun to sit right up at the front, or did they call it near the nose?

She noticed that there was a cream curtain drawn across this forward section, and the half dozen seats on the other side seemed more luxurious, rather like spaciously designed armchairs. All the better! She plumped down in one, passing judgement on the upholstery with a pleased sigh.

The stewardess at this end was out at the open door beside the flight deck. She was engrossed in watching a woman in a wheelchair being guided across the tarmac from a black car towards the boarding steps. From her seat beside the window Janet had a good view of the discussion that was taking place as the stewardess went down to give some assistance.

She saw another sleek black car glide up. Who should step out from the door that was speedily opened for him but the man with the pigskin luggage whom she had seen earlier near the weigh-in section. She cast a disinterested glance over his immaculately tailored suit, then returned wide-eyed to the intriguing article she had been reading in her magazine. It was all about a woman who had gone out to study the habits of the deadly piranha fish in the rivers of the Brazilian jungle. The adventuress was explaining what happened after the boat she was paddling hit a rock, when

15

Janet heard a deep crisp voice slicing metallically through her suspense with, 'I believe you're sitting in my seat.'

She looked up to find the man who had just stepped out of the car hovering beside her.

His seat! She glared at him. As far as she knew, all the other passengers who had come on to the plane behind her had been content to take what they could. 'There are plenty more around,' she flashed at him coldly. 'I don't see why I should move when I was here first.'

The man's blue eyes had the gleam of chipped ice. He straightened his lean frame and turning sat down in a chair across the aisle. Without another glance in her direction he crossed one immaculately trousered leg over the other and opening the slim briefcase he had with him, he began to flick through a sheaf of papers.

Janet returned haughtily to her magazine. Well, that had put *him* in his place! She would have liked to lose herself again in the world of the Brazilian jungle, but her emotions at the slight brush were flying up in her chest like caged butterflies. She found herself staring at the words without taking in their meaning.

Her attention wandered to the open doorway where the woman in the wheelchair was now being transported inside. There was an elderly man with her with beautiful white hair and a clipped moustache. An expensively groomed couple came in after them. The stewardess, whose main concern was the woman in the wheelchair, hurried inside amongst the group.

Her gaze flew instantly to Janet. Under a tiny frown it swung with some dismay on to the man who was engrossed in his briefcase papers. She stepped briskly forward and with a perfect smile she bent and asked Janet in the lightest of whispered tones if she could see her air ticket.

Janet obliged, and charmingly the stewardess smiled, 'Ah yes, Miss Kendall. We have a seat for you back here.' She parted the cream curtains beckoningly, and realising now that they were there for a reason, Janet fumbled for her things, colouring furiously.

Discreetly looking past her embarrassment, the stewardess moved in to seek the attention of the man with the briefcase. Gesturing him forward, she murmured, profoundly apologetic, 'I'm terribly sorry, sir. I really don't know how that happened. I've been rather occupied seeing to these other first class passengers. . .'

'That's all right. Don't worry about it.' The man relaxed his rather well-shaped mouth and rose. He moved across the aisle and sat down in the seat that Janet had just vacated, not letting his icy blue gaze stray from his papers. Janet dived through the curtain feeling small enough to have crawled through under the carpet.

The main section of the plane was quite full, but there were one or two vacant places near at hand. 'Here you are. You can still have a seat near the window.' The stewardess came smilingly up behind her. She helped her to settle in and fastening her seat belt told her pleasantly, 'We'll be coming round with drinks just after take-off, if you'd like one?'

Thanks to her expertise Janet was put quickly at her ease. But long after the plane had left the ground, and the clouds were rushing past the window like smoke, she felt the superior presence of the flinty-eyed man on the other side of the curtain so forcefully there might have been no division between them.

Two pink spots in her cheeks, she turned her attention resolutely to the wonders of flying. Well, he needn't think *she* cared one way or the other about his stuffy old chair!

CHAPTER TWO

THE clouds dispersed and Janet got a glimpse of a grey ocean way, way down below. She was brave enough to pick out the tiny white-capped waves for a while, but when the sun projected the plane's shadow on the sea, her heart gave a tiny lurch and she had to bring her glance inside again.

A light tea was served half way through the journey. When she looked out again, they were flying over the Pyrenees. She stared down fascinated on mile upon mile of snow-capped mountains. From up here they looked like jagged whisked-up peaks of icing on a huge cake.

Later she was able to pick out the speckle of hamlets set in a green countryside until they were shut out by a solid bank of cloud that lay under the plane, thick and cumulus and grey, and shot with the pink light of late afternoon.

Just after five o'clock, the pilot announced over the speakers that they were approaching Ibiza and would be landing in ten minutes. Janet fastened her seat belt and felt another lurch of her heart as the engines changed rhythm and the plane nosed down through the clouds.

Presently through the mist she saw the island just as she remembered it from last time, its craggy mountains and white-waved inlets growing ever clearer as the jet lost height.

They thundered in towards the airport and hopefully she tried to pick out her mother's tiny house, but everything was a whirl of green fields, white villages, and winding roads. Before she knew it squat windmills were spinning away past the windows and the wheels were touching down on the runway.

For a while there was nothing to be heard but the scream

18

of the engines and the roar of the tyres over the ground as they streaked along like the wind. Then gradually their speed slackened and the airport buildings came into view.

The moment the wheels stopped and the engines were shut off the inside of the plane became alive. People chattered and reached for hand luggage and searched for outer garments. The stewardesses moved up and down the aisle giving assistance where they could.

Janet filed out amidst the crush, turning her back on the cream curtain and not giving it another thought. Outside the buses were waiting to take them across the short space of tarmac. Struck by the balmy warmth in the air and the mingled scents of the countryside which were so different from England, she found a place and a few minutes later stepped down at the passenger terminal. Inside the pillared area there was that clamorous, slightly melancholic atmosphere that always pervades a spot where people are constantly coming and going. Passengers were weaving at all angles across the open space, and uniformed porters, Ibicencos with dark eyes and swarthy smiling faces, trundled their trolleys around shouting, 'Allo! Allo!' not as a form of greeting as Janet had at first thought, but to point out that they were at liberty to transport your luggage.

When at last her own cases turned up on the conveyor belt, she preferred to save the pesetas it would have cost her and tugged outside with them herself. The taxis were not very abundant. And what there were, their drivers were in no hurry to secure themselves a fare.

As Janet expected, when she gained the attention of one of them, his face dropped when she told him the distance she wanted to go. None of them were eager to accept country journeys. They liked to drop their fares quickly at some nearby hotel or villa and return to the animated chat that went on amidst their groups outside the airport lounges. Money didn't come into it. They were indolent, and they preferred their indolence to getting rich.

19

Janet stood firm and willed her driver to swing her cases into his car. Once they were out on to the Ibizan highway he accepted his fate with the happy resignation of his race and began to sing flamenco at the top of his voice.

Thus serenaded, Janet got her first view on this trip of the island. It was something to take the breath away even at this twilight hour. Though dusk was well on its way the sky was still a deep clear blue, and from it a full round moon shone with incredible brilliance. This unusual light gave the fields and trees a vivid emerald green look and the white cube-like houses dotted around gleamed like torches.

The road took them through the town of Ibiza with its narrow streets and sandstone cathedral which she remembered from her last visit. From here they followed the main highway through the country for a while, later coming out on to the coast route that ran past the beaches of Santa Eulalia and various other little coves. The view now, caught in glimpses every once in a while, was of a moonlit sea stretching silently away from the land in a ripple of silver.

When the taxi turned off into the countryside again Janet armed herself with her directions. Though San Gabrielle, the name of the village they were making for, was familiar to most of the islanders, when it came to the tucked-away situation of her mother's house she knew more than they did.

The village turned up in due course and pointing ahead she urged the driver all the way through it and out on to the road again at the other side. As he cruised along uncertainly she kept her eyes peeled for the huge spreading carob tree that marked the entrance to a lesser known track. As she remembered it, it was about a ten-minute walk out of the village. And sure enough there it was coming up ahead.

The good-natured Ibizan's face dropped again when he saw the pitted road down which he was expected to take his beautiful taxi. He turned in gallantly, however, and felt his way as though he was driving on eggs.

Janet gazed out at the familiar sights of almond groves and farm fields spread out in ghostly stillness under the full moon. She could see the whitewashed walls of the farm on a slightly raised hill ahead in the distance, and the village they had just passed through on another hill to her right.

As the car crunched steadily along she kept a careful watch. Eventually the imposing pink bulk of the villa showed up. Throughout her fortnight's holiday here two years ago the place had been shuttered and unoccupied and she had never given it a thought. Now she rode past it with a certain rebellious apprehension. Lights blazed and people were living there. People who were trying to cheat her mother out of what rightfully belonged to her.

To give a boost to her flagging morale she wasted no time when the disused railway track showed itself in a dim grey line cutting across the road in front of them to continue on past the side of the villa. With a proprietorial air she directed the taxi man to turn in on what, as far as she was concerned, was her mother's drive. He winced at the temporary surface of small rocks, but swung in obligingly and drove up grandly alongside the small white Ibizan house to where the light was streaming from the front door.

Even before they were half way along the drive Janet heard the excited barking of Dale, her mother's little dog. Arriving and opening the car door, she was overwhelmed by canine affection. Then her mother was hurrying out to hug her amidst a stream of high-pitched chatter. Janet had to let much of this go by the board while she paid the taxi man, who being of the Spanish race, and family lovers all, was eyeing the scene with a sly gleam of indulgence.

She gave him the required amount and handed him a good tip for his help. He accepted smilingly but without being ingratiating, and with a polite, 'Adios, señorita,' and to her mother, 'Adios, señora,' he stepped into his car and turning flamboyantly on the small area of terrace beside the house, he crunched away down the track.

21

Janet picked up her cases and followed her mother inside. She stepped straight into a pleasantly lit room, and continued through with Dale fussing at her heels, to the spare bedroom across a small hallway. Pushing the door open for her, her mother, beaming on her affectionately, turned away and said fussily, 'I'll go and see about your supper. You must be famished.'

Janet caught her before she went and gave her a mischievous hug. She felt the face against hers, soft and papery smooth, and smelt the lingering air of violets, just as she always remembered her. With a rush of love she planted a kiss on her cheek, then turned inside to unpack.

It was a pretty bedroom, uncluttered and designed for coolness. The floor was chequered in big black and white tiles, and the twin bed coverlets with gathered frills around the sides were in the palest green. The drapes which hung from ceiling to floor across the one wall of windows were patterned with huge white camellias on a slightly deeper green background. The walls were in eggshell blue.

She remembered the room from sharing it with Nona on their holiday visit. Now that she had it to herself, she made full use of the wardrobe and drawers which were in neutral wood. She had no idea how long she would have to stay, but in any case her clothes might as well have a good home while she was here.

Since she had only brought light summer wear the job of unpacking was soon completed. After going along to the bathroom to freshen up with a quick wash she made her way back to the living room.

Though designed on Spanish lines with its wide fire place, the tiled chimneypiece tapering up to the ceiling, and its small windows, the Kendall stamp on the room was unmistakable in the framed family photographs, the big chintzy cushions, Dale's crochet-cushioned dog-basket and the well worn English rugs.

Wandering round in the glow of red-shaded table

lamps, fingering ornaments and trinkets and oddments in furniture that she associated with her childhood, Janet felt a warm glow. This was home. Truly home.

Her mother called her from the kitchen which was through a door at the far side of the room. Where formica table and chairs formed a compact eating space in the small area Janet wasted no time in alleviating her hunger. Though the Spanish food her mother had prepared for her tasted strange after the English diet she was used to, she enjoyed it tremendously.

Saving her chatter and the questions she was bursting to ask about the rest of her family, Mrs Kendall plied her daughter with everything she could lay her hands on to eat, as mothers will.

'Have some more pimientos, dear. You might as well finish them off.' And, 'I can cut you some more *sobrada* if you like.'

'Mummy darling, I'm not a horse!' Janet teased her laughingly, escaping from the table. Arm in arm they walked into the living room. The air was warm, but just to give a welcoming touch Mrs Kendall had one log glowing away to itself in the fireplace. Dale, long since worn out with all the excitement, was curled up in his basket fast asleep.

Janet pulled up an old leather pouffe beside the family armchair and spent the next half hour putting her mother's mind at rest on the usual spate of domestic enquiries.

No, her brother Ian wasn't going to have to leave his wife and family to work in Brussels. Someone else had been found to take his place and this would in no way impair his own chances for promotion with his firm. And yes, her sister's baby, little Emma, was now quite over the croup she'd had, and Adrian, another grandchild, would be starting school after the Easter holidays.

Mrs Kendall, her animated features working happily, soaked up every word of news. She was an attractive

23

woman in a faded way, with a greying auburn fringe frizzed across her forehead and eyes that were lit constantly with the sparkle of humour. She had a habit of chattering on about nonsensical things when no one was listening and she would frequently intersperse her prattle with nerve-jangling tinkles of laughter. But her heart was warm, and there was no one she wouldn't help.

When at last she was sated with family chat, Janet let a reasonable silence elapse. Then broaching the all-important subject, she asked in business-like tones, 'Now, what about these people next door? Tell me about them.'

'Well, dear, there's nothing much to tell,' Mrs Kendall said, then immediately went into a long discourse on the history of the previous owners. 'As you know, Mr and Mrs Weston had to sell. Such a nice couple they were. The husband was a diamond merchant, I believe, and they had houses all over the place. They had this one built, you know, so that they could supervise the building of the villa, and they let me have it without a penny profit to themselves. They really were wonderful people, though I didn't see much of them . . .'

Realising by her daughter's good-natured frown that she was in danger of digressing, she pulled herself up and started again. 'Well, apparently the poor man has contracted heart trouble of some kind and he's been told that it would be very dangerous to travel. So they've sold all their property abroad and settled in England.'

'And what about the new owners of the villa?' Janet steered the conversation on to a firm footing. 'Have you met them?'

'Oh yes!' Mrs Kendall said chirpily. 'A Mr Ralph Ford, and his wife . . . Elspeth, or Esmeralda or something. They're very rich. He's to do with shipping, so they say. They've got several friends staying with them at the moment, and then there are all these other people they know. They come rolling up in these madly expensive cars—

brought over from the mainland, I suppose—and park them all along the drive.'

'But haven't you complained?' Janet asked indignantly.

'Well, yes!' Mrs Kendall's eyes were wide and round. 'I told them it was very awkward when I was expecting my delivery of Butano—you know, the gas they use over here —or if the water man had to back his wagon up to the well.'

'And what did they say to that?' Janet asked, tightening her mouth.

'Oh, Mr Ford said that they'd been given to understand that the strip of track went with the property. And as he needed it for his guests he would have to look further into his rights to make it an adjoining drive to the villa. Oh, he was very nice about it!' Mrs Kendall hastened to add. 'Everyone has been pleasantness itelf.'

'Well, they would be, wouldn't they?' Janet retorted, her cheeks aflame. 'They obviously think you're going to sit back and do nothing about it.'

Her mother shrugged and gave a light sigh, and said nothing, which was a sure pointer to Janet that she hadn't really given it much thought.

She pressed ahead grimly with, 'How long have they been here, the new people?'

'Oh, only two or three weeks,' Mrs Kendall chirruped on again. 'The first I knew that the villa had changed hands was when the lorries were outside at the front . . . I couldn't see a lot from here, but they'd be bringing in their personal stuff, I expect. I happen to know that the Westons sold the place as it was, lock, stock, and barrel . . . it's beautifully furnished, I believe, Spanish decor throughout, you know, and expensive pieces . . . I haven't been in there myself, but that's what I've heard. And of course, the grounds were already mature. They simply knocked down the old villa that was standing and put a new one in its place.'

'Wasn't it the Westons, the previous owners, who told

you you would be able to buy the track?' Janet asked, curbing her mother's ramblings.

'Yes, they weren't interested in it themselves. They didn't entertain all that much and what cars there were they parked inside their front entrance. They told me that it was used years ago to transport salt—the old railway track, I mean—and it belonged to the government, or something. And when they got round to it, it was going to be parcelled out and sold very cheaply to the people whose land adjoined it.'

'Mmmm!' Janet mused on her mother's words and replied with a measure of satisfaction. 'Well, your land adjoins this section.'

'I know, dear, but so does the villa's,' Mrs Kendall said, not lacking in logic.

'Yes, but your house fronts on to it,' Janet argued. 'Theirs doesn't.'

'No,' her mother agreed, looking thoughtful. 'The Westons had it built this way so that they could keep an eye on the workmen at the villa.'

Janet sighed. 'I don't suppose they knew what a problem they were creating,' she said darkly.

'Oh, I'm sure they didn't.' Mrs Kendall rushed to their defence. 'They always regarded it as my drive. I don't know that I ever saw them come up the track once—you know, to the side entrance into their grounds, the big double gateway across from here—but the new people use it all the time.'

'They've probably found out it belongs to no one yet, so they think they might as well have it as anyone else,' Janet said, her mouth tightening up again.

'I expect that's it, dear.' Mrs Kendall, sighing, was plainly becoming bored with the subject.

Janet rallied her with the stirring words, 'Well, we mustn't let them. If they were allowed to buy up this section of track your house would be worthless without an entrance. And I don't intend to stand by and watch that happen.'

Mrs Kendall sighed again and murmured, her attention wandering, 'But I'm not sure I know what we can do about it.'

'Well, the Westons must have made some enquiries about buying the track somewhere to have got the information they did?' Janet pondered, frowning.

'Oh yes! They told me they'd talked with the mayor in San Gabrielle,' her mother recalled. 'Apparently each section comes under the jurisdiction of its nearest village.'

'That's it, then. We'll take it from there,' Janet said cheerfully. 'If the Westons put a claim in while they were living in this house, then it should be going on. All we have to do is stir them up a bit in the village and let them know that it's important that you have this strip for your drive.'

'All right, Jan dear. If you think that's best.'

Seeing her mother's puckered features and uncertain look, Janet hugged her reassuringly. 'Now don't worry. I'll do all that's necessary. You needn't bother about a thing,' she said confidently.

'But these things take time.' The worn hands fiddled with the covers of the chair.

'That doesn't matter.' Janet dropped a kiss on the faded cheek. 'I've cancelled my holiday to Greece and I've enough money to supplement the housekeeping for as long as I'm here.'

'You are a pet to do all that for me.' Her mother's smile returned. Then, eager to dispense with the subject, she exclaimed brightly, 'Now, how would you like a nice warm drink before bed?'

Later lying between the sheets, listening to the strange calls of the night birds, on a silence which was odd to her ears after the continuous roar of London, Janet thought of her mother and her reaction to the conversation they had had. Gentle natured and of a carefree disposition, she hated

27

trouble. And she had never been one for putting up a fight.

But she, Janet, was, and she intended to do just that to see that her mother got a fair deal in this business over the track.

She awoke to the familiar sounds of those gay twittering tones as the bedroom door was opened and a tray appeared. 'Breakfast!' Her mother, looking as fresh as paint in a bright flowered apron, stepped fussily in and approached the bed.

Janet sat up abruptly, her glance flying to the clock beside her. It was after nine. 'Mother!' she smiled reproachfully at the tray and scolded gently. 'You ought to have got me up.'

She had a fresh boiled egg, buttered toast, and tea placed regally before her with the affectionate reply. 'I knew you'd be tired after travelling, so I thought I'd let you sleep in a bit. Besides, it's nice to have someone to spoil.'

Propped up against the pillows and dipping fingers of toast, Janet thought she had never tasted eggs like this in the city. The big yellow shutters at the windows were closed, but the sun found its way through the slits, illuminating the room with a warm morning glow.

And wasn't it wonderful to be able to sit up in sleeveless cotton nightdress and not have to make a rush for woollen bedjacket. The air itself was like velvet around her bare arms.

She sipped the imported English tea and basked in the pleasures of being idle, becoming aware gradually that her mother was hanging about, straightening the bed cover, flicking the curtains, and re-setting the lace mats on the dressing table in a way that she did when she was bursting with some piece of news.

Janet waited, and eventually her mother said, patting the pillows for the twentieth time, 'I hear a new guest arrived at the villa last night.'

28

Was *that* all? Janet smiled over her egg and teased lightly, 'I didn't know you were that well up in the language to join in the local gossip.' From what she knew of her mother's Spanish she could understand enough to get by on, but she hadn't the capacity to start learning it at her age.

'I'm not,' Mrs Kendall acknowledged wryly. 'Juana, a woman from the village, works at the villa, and she's picked up quite a bit of English. I see her sometimes when she's shaking the rugs over the wall.'

She straightened the tea pot daintily on the tray and re-positioned a knife, and when a suitable time had elapsed, she asked with something of a flutter, 'Guess who the new arrival is?'

'I haven't a clue.' Janet bit on her last finger of toast with tolerant amusement.

Her mother fussed to pour her a second cup of tea, then all a-twitter she leaned in to tell her with a mixture of awe and excitement. 'Mr Bruce Walbrook.' And when Janet's face didn't immediately register the same awe and surprise she cried, '*You know! Bruce Walbrook*, the well-known lawyer. He's quite a big name in England.'

Janet thought about it and said vaguely, 'Yes, I think I've heard of him ... a lawyer, you say?' Her glance suddenly sharpened as she looked at her mother. 'What's he doing at the villa? Holidaying, do you think?'

'No.' Her mother mouthed her suspicions in tones piquantly intrigued. 'It's my guess Ralph Ford has got him over to work on their claim to the track. I remember his very words were that he would have to look further into his rights, and rich people always employ lawyers, don't they?'

'But it doesn't always get them anywhere,' Janet said undaunted. She finished her tea and handed the tray back, voicing her thoughts with a rebellious light. 'Lawyer or no lawyer, he'll still have to take his turn in the queue.'

She stepped out of bed and stretched luxuriously, and

29

Mrs Kendall, her excitement fast melting away, went off humming to herself in her gay detached manner.

Janet went to take a shower, later reviewing this new situation which had arisen, in her room. But after she had donned flowered blouse and vivid slacks she turned towards the outdoors, dismissing the subject from her mind. From what she knew of her mother's life out here, official matters had a habit of taking their time. It wasn't likely that the presence of an eminent British lawyer would make the Ibicencos move any faster.

The sun was surprisingly hot when she stepped out on to the front patio and wandered on to the surrounding terrace. The incredible beauty of the scene struck at her heart as it always did each time she gazed on it. It was easy to see why the Westons had chosen to build here.

The close proximity of pine-clad mountains, their craggy peaks outlined against a sparkling blue sky, provided a dramatic backcloth to the Moorish-type farmhouse standing on its small hill to the left of the house. Where the patio looked down the track towards the farm road, which ran past the front garden, green cultivated fields took the eye across to the other hill where the white cube-like dwellings of San Gabrielle clustered closely together around its slopes. And to add to the Moorish flavour of the scene, on the right of the house on the other side of the track were the three huge date palms which grew inside the villa grounds, their heavy green fronds contrasting darkly with the blue of the sky.

Janet dragged her gaze away from the setting, and getting down to business, studied her mother's house.

Smooth-walled and flat-roofed, it was L-shaped in design, the living room with its three sets of yellow shuttered windows being the projection that looked out on to the track, and her mother's bedroom jutting out at right angles to face on to the front garden. The spare bedroom, the one that Janet was using at the moment, the bathroom and the

30

kitchen, made up the rest of the shape at the back.

The house stood close to the farm road in a long strip of meadow which stretched alongside the track. Apart from a tumbledown old field wall which fronted the garden at the roadside and two short lengths of chicken wire up as far as the terrace on each side to keep Dale from roaming, her mother's strip of land had nothing to distinguish it from the surrounding farm fields.

She took her gaze over to the villa, its high pink walls running parallel with the track on the opposite side and encompassing an area of ground the same length as her mother's meadow. She could see the big old Spanish gateway set in the wall across the track from here. This was the side entrance to the villa. She knew there was a similar imposing entrance at the front, which opened on to the farm road.

Janet brought her gaze back in to study her mother's house. She had to admit that the front door, set in the corner of the L-shaped square of patio, looked out on to the garden and the farm road, the same as the villa did, but it was obvious the house had been designed to incorporate the track as a drive. Anyone could see that at a glance.

Satisfied with her observations, she came in at last from the small terrace that surrounded the house.

Dale had been fussing around her delightedly ever since she had stepped out of doors. She patted him and played with him now, and chased him on to the patio. Her mother was watering the numerous pots that she kept along one side of it. She had a passion for growing things. She was training a sprig of jasmine to climb up round the doorway, and a similar sprig of bougainvillaea was creeping up the corner of the living-room wall. She had a rose bush flourishing in an old green pot besides velvet-leaved geraniums, and the grapevine she had planted two years ago at the corner pillar of the patio was now stretching leafy arms across the loggia above.

31

She hadn't been able to do much with the garden because it was too big an area for her to manage. But it was attractive in a haphazard way with the dark summer greenery of oleander and hibiscus bushes waving everywhere and clumps of wallflowers dotted amongst islands of marigolds and summer stocks. The whole of this front area of the house was dominated by two enormous fig trees.

There were two cane rocking chairs on the patio. With a view to taking a seat Janet turned, and noticing for the first time the furry shape stretched out on the cushion of one of them she exclaimed to her mother, 'I didn't know you had a cat!'

'I got her from the farm.' Mrs Kendall raised herself and watched affectionately as Janet picked up the bundle to stroke it. 'They were going to drown half a dozen unwanted kittens, so I thought I must save at least one of them.' She gave a little burst of her pattering laughter as she explained, 'She was so tall and leggy at two months, I christened her Twiggy.'

'Very apt.' Janet smiled as the cat jumped down to pad with curiosity around her.

She was very slim with a small head and ears, and eyes that were large and yellow. Her fur, from the crown of her head to the tip of her tail, was pale orange striped with darker tones. Her face and her four incredibly long legs and undersides were a beautiful snowy white.

'She's eight months old now,' Mrs Kendall emptied her watering can on the last of the plants. 'She's turned out to be a dear little thing, and she's handy for keeping the field-mice off the patio.'

'Help!' Janet said laughingly, lifting her gaze.

At the same time her mother stretched up from her task and together they noticed the figure which had appeared round the corner from the front of the villa and was now strolling leisurely up the track.

It was a man, lean of frame and tallish. Though he was

32

casually dressed in cream slacks, white shirt, a dark patterned cravat at his throat, it was obvious even at a distance that he dealt only with the best tailors.

A guest from the villa, undoubtedly. Janet would have turned away then, but something about the autocratic bearing, the inflexible line of the lean jaw, made her gaze become riveted on him. As he came nearer an awful realisation flashed across her mind. She said to her mother, quickly under her breath,

'That man—who is he? Do you know?'

Mrs Kendall, her face bright with recognition, recalling probably some old newspaper photograph, breathed, 'Why, yes, that's him! That's the man I told you about, dear. The lawyer who arrived at the villa last night.'

Catching sight of a flinty blue gaze, the same one that had frozen her in her seat, or rather, his seat on the plane, and then watched with odious satisfaction as she was removed from it for his benefit, Janet hissed, sending a venomous look his way, 'You don't mean to say *he's* Bruce Walbrook?'

CHAPTER THREE

Mrs Kendall was too busy offering polite smiles and nods across the patio to bother with a reply. Not that Janet needed one. She had felt from the start that the man was an enemy. She was more than convinced of the fact now.

She heard those crisp deep tones once more as he greeted briskly while strolling, 'Good morning to you. It's a beautiful day.'

'Good morning!' Mrs Kendall called back gaily. 'Yes, it is a lovely day.'

Janet, who was having none of his austere charm and chat, swung contemptuously away, and on a pretext of taking Dale for a run directed her steps quickly towards the back meadow. It was simply a matter of following the terrace round to the back of the house, then taking the winding path that started at its centre.

The path led down as far as the big old almond tree which marked the boundary of her mother's property. She kept her eyes on the tree, chattering lightly to Dale, who romped ahead, while coping with the burning in her cheeks after her encounter with a man she had fervently hoped she would never see again. She pulled a wry face when she recalled now her ignorance of his motives for being on the plane. Not only was he going to stay right next door to her mother's house here in Ibiza, but he had come over for the express purpose of gaining ownership of the track for the people at the villa.

Her brown eyes flashed as she moved rapidly away from the house and the suave greeting he had offered just now. He needn't think *she* was going to act as though it was just a friendly fight!

She arrived at the small paddock at the bottom of the meadow, with its higgledy-piggledy hutches and stalls, where her mother kept various livestock to supplement the food table. Hens fluttered and clucked about inside the wire netting, colliding with padding cackling ducks. There was a small goat tethered to a grass patch where it stood munching happily, and a family of white rabbits sat fat and round, blinking contentedly in the sun.

While she was down here Janet thought she might as well have a look to see if there were any eggs about. Leaving Dale outside sniffing around the grass, she pushed aside the makeshift gate and leaned it back into place behind her. There was an old enamelled basin on one of the shelves near by. With this in hand she scouted around amongst indignant squawks from the hens and searched out three beautiful dark brown eggs. She lined the basin with a little straw to keep them safe and went on to give the goat a pat on its bony sides.

In a lean-to shed at the end of the paddock was all the clutter that her mother didn't care to have about the house, but couldn't bear to part with either. There was a very shabby grandfather clock, an old carpet sweeper, endless brooms, a disused gas fire, a broken sewing machine, and a dozen more objects that were lost in the gloom.

What caught Janet's eye was the low-wheeled modern-type bicycle which her mother had used for shopping in England. She had brought it out with her to use for the same purpose in Ibiza, but obviously the idea had been short-lived.

After a few moments' poking around Janet left the paddock and, bowl of eggs in hand, closed the gate behind her. She looked around for Dale. She had only left him for a few minutes, but he was nowhere to be seen. Her heart missed a beat when she thought of him wandering away from the unfenced meadow. Then she saw him. He was off to the side of her, on the track, making himself disgustingly friendly with the detestable Mr Walbrook.

'Dale, come here at once!' she called crossly, afraid to walk too quickly in case she broke the eggs. The little dog, much like a Cairn to look at but with the curling shaggy white hair of a poodle, ignored her completely and continued to nuzzle with tail-wagging affection the hand that reached down to him.

Janet quickened her steps, maddened by his disobedience. Perhaps sensing some of her ill-humour in the way she moved, Dale tore himself away at last and scuttled back to his own strip of field.

His reluctance to come when called had taken Janet almost on to the track. With him romping in front of her, she was preparing to wheel away, ignoring the lean figure framed against the pink walls of the villa grounds, when the blue eyes smote her icily, and the crisp voice clipped, 'I see your manners haven't improved.'

Janet had the grace to blush then, for she knew that she had been rude to him on more than one occasion. But it only angered her more to have to admit it, and staying to confront him she flared acidly, 'If you mean because I didn't stand cooing "good morning" to you at the house just now when I know why you're here, no, they haven't.'

It was obvious he was out for the sole purpose of weighing up the position of the disused railway track and the two properties. Flicking his gaze in from where it roamed over the villa walls, he said caustically, 'Perhaps we'd better introduce ourselves. I'm Bruce Walbrook. And as you've already stated, you know why I'm here.'

Janet drew herself up, bowl of eggs and all, and displaying her awareness she flashed back, 'I'm Janet Kendall, and you might as well know that I'm here for the same reason. I don't intend to stand by and watch my mother cheated out of what rightfully belongs to her.'

'I think we'll leave such words as cheating out of our vocabulary, shall we, Miss Kendall?' His voice was like the rustling of ice on a glacier stream.

In his wig and gown, or whatever it was lawyers wore, Janet could well imagine being frozen to the spot by his courtroom asperity. However, she was not on the witness stand, and brushing aside her qualms she retorted, 'What else would you call it? Perhaps you don't know that my mother has had first claim to this strip of track for the two years that she's lived alongside it. The Fords only arrived a few weeks ago. How can they expect to have any rights to it?'

'To put you into the legal picture, Miss Kendall,' a flicker of smiling scorn passed over the carved features, 'your mother's strip of land was once part of villa property. Her house which the Westons chose to build on the other side of the track is but a recent addition, which automatically puts it in second place, where claims are concerned, with the villa, which has stood for more than a century.'

'The old villa, yes!' Janet replied unmoved, 'but that's been knocked down.'

'In point of law that makes no difference.'

Goaded on by his smooth rejoinder, Janet scoffed in his face, 'Whose law? Certainly not here in Ibiza. My mother has Mr Weston's word that her house was designed to include the track as a drive. And that's the way he arranged it with the authorities in the village.'

Bruce Walbrook gave her a deprecating smile and taking it down to his immaculate shoes he warned in his precise tones, 'I shouldn't depend on that if I were you. Arrangements have a habit of falling by the wayside in these places.'

'Precisely,' Janet fired back. 'So there's no reason for you to be optimistic either, is there?'

Marvelling at her nerve under the stringent blue gaze, she gave him a thin smile in return.

He fixed her with a steely look, then turning his attention along the track he said with a gesture of impatience, 'I fail to see why such a small house needs a drive at all. It seems to me your mother could have some access made in from the farm road in the old wall fronting her garden. There's room inside to allow for a parking area.'

'The same might be said of the villa.' Janet seethed at the colossal high-handedness of the man. Calmly lowering the value of her mother's property to the tune of hundreds of pounds!

'The villa grounds are largely ornamented,' he said icily. 'There is one small drive in from the gate. As the Fords are used to entertaining considerably, this is quite inadequate.'

'And I suppose that's a good enough reason for encroaching on a widow's property,' Janet tossed at him shrewishly.

'The track belongs to no one yet, Miss Kendall,' he said harshly.

Janet didn't care that his eyes held that glacial gleam of his profession again. She tossed her head at him and snapped, 'Well, as far as I'm concerned it belongs to my mother, and I intend to do all that I can to see that she gets it.'

Her glance crossing swords with his, he smiled his cold legal smile and inclining his lean frame in a disparaging shrug he stated, 'It's as well to know where we stand.' As Dale, tired of sniffing around by this time, set up an impatient yapping, he terminated the conversation with a brisk, 'Good day to you, Miss Kendall.'

'Good day to *you*, Mr Walbrook.' Janet smiled acidly and turning, she walked off with the romping dog at her heels.

Emotionally strung up after their verbal battle, she followed the winding path up the centre of her mother's strip of meadow, only too aware that Bruce Walbrook was moving on a parallel with her, back the way he had come along the track. She gave no indication of her banging heart or quivering nerves, but talked gaily to Dale and teased him laughingly with the bowl of eggs she held over him. There was a door at the rear of the house, and wasting no time crossing the back terrace she escaped on her trembling legs inside.

Her mother was beating something up in the kitchen. She sang out in her carefree, detached way as Janet went by, 'What were you talking to Mr Walbrook about, dear?'

'Oh, just putting him in the picture, as regards the track,' Janet called back nonchalantly. She waited until her legs had stopped shaking, then sailed in to explain, 'I was telling him we wouldn't be agreeing to anything except one hundred per cent ownership.'

But her mother had forgotten already that she had asked the question, and busying herself between oven and table she espied the eggs Janet had brought in, and exclaimed, 'Oh, I'm so glad you found some more, dear. I thought I'd make *huevos al plato* for lunch. What do you think?'

'Well, seeing that I don't know what they are, let's just say that I'll chance it,' Janet laughed, relieved to be able to lose herself in domestic chat. However, though she took a hand lightheartedly in the preparation, and hummed to herself as she laid the table, it was over the tumultuous knowledge inside her that the fight for the track was really on. After her clash with Bruce Walbrook just now there was no doubt about that. Thinking of him she was seized with a fierce desire to rush out and do something to outstrip him, instead of calmly setting out knives and forks. He was sure to be putting some plan into motion. On edge at the mere thought of it, she felt like a runner in a race, straining behind the starting tape, to get away before her opponent.

Unable to contain her desperation, she said to her mother as casually as she could over lunch, 'By the way, I saw your bicycle down in the shed. Don't you use it now?'

'I find I don't need it.' Mrs Kendall poured two glasses of water from the carafe on the table. 'Miguel from the farm stops by with my bread and milk and any odd thing I want from the village, and I take the bus to do my weekly shopping in town.' Her hands fluttering about from one thing to another it occurred to her to follow up the question with, 'Why do you ask, dear?'

'Oh, I thought I'd use it for transport while I'm here. If you don't need it.' Janet shrugged, and as her mother nodded her approval, she went on, 'Actually, I thought I'd cycle up to the village straight after lunch, and see if I can have a talk with the mayor.'

Mrs Kendall pulled her daughter up with an amused light, reminding her, 'This is Ibiza, Jan. Nothing stirs in the village till after four. Even the church clock goes to sleep.' She laughed as she helped herself to more salad. 'They have to keep starting it up around tea time.'

Botheration! Janet sipped on her water meditatively. She had forgotten all about the siesta period. That meant more waiting around before she could do anything.

However, determined to make use of the time in which she was compelled to cool her heels, she helped with the dishes, then settled at the table in the living room with a writing pad and her Spanish phrase book.

While she battled through the afternoon memorising such sentences as, *'Where is the town hall?'*—*'I wish to see the mayor,'* the rest of the household succumbed to the Spanish way of life. Her mother dozed on her bed in her shuttered bedroom, Dale slept with his paws in the air in his basket, a contented smile on his face, and Twiggy stretched luxuriously on her chair in the sun.

Janet wandered out there occasionally, testing herself without the aid of the Spanish book, on what she had rehearsed over and over again. All was quiet over at the villa. She wondered ominously what Bruce Walbrook was up to. It occurred to her to realise that there was nothing he *could* do, except go and see the mayor, as she was doing.

In a fever lest he should beat her to it, she went in and freshened up quickly with a wash and touch of make-up, even though it was only half past three, and hurrying down the meadow she wheeled out the bicycle.

It would have been less bumpy to wheel it back up the path as far as the house, but she chose the rocky track so as not to disturb Dale into a frenzy of excited yapping. She stepped as quietly as she could past the patio and the open front door and mounting when she got to the farm road, she pedalled silently off.

The big front gates of the villa were open as she passed, but there was nothing to be glimpsed, except a mass of luxuriant greenery and one or two cars parked close together inside.

The countryside was enveloped in that same sleepy silence she had left behind at the house. All the sound seemed to have been sucked away to beat back like a faint whisper from the far horizons. Only the occasional buzz of an insect, the lethargic cheep of a bird, could be heard on the still air around the almond groves.

Up on the main road the tyres of the bicycle added a dull swish as they spun over the asphalt. Though it was only April, Janet was startled at the heat of the sun. It beat down on her bare head, and gave a glare to the white road that hurt her eyes. She made a mental note to buy a shady hat and sun-glasses at the first opportunity.

Coming into the village it became necessary to pedal harder because of the steep rise uphill. In the end she had to give it up, and pushing the bike the rest of the way, she left it at the bottom of a sloping street to pick up on her return.

There wasn't a soul to be seen. She might have cycled into a ghost town. The houses, where the sun struck down between the narrowness of the alleys, were boarded and shuttered as though never to be opened again. Staring about her, as she walked a little apprehensive in the silence, it didn't occur to Janet to turn. When she did so accidentally, she was taken unawares by the fantastic view.

It ought to have dawned on her that, climbing as she had been all the time, there might be something like this over her shoulder. Instead, finding the whole plain clear up to the foot of the mountains spread out below her came as a delightful shock.

Out where a grassy platform ran between two houses she stood poised on a hillock, to drink in the view. She could see the ribbon of farm road and her mother's tiny white house beside the pink palm-shrouded block of the villa. She could see the farm perched on its little hill, and in the distance, within the sheltered slopes of the foothills, and dotted across the open plain, were the tiny white clusters of villages, like San Gabrielle.

She turned away at last, amused to think that she had spent a whole two weeks here once without knowing that such a view existed.

Her scant knowledge of Ibizan villages told her that there would be a main square somewhere which would probably house the civic buildings. She found the Plaza de España at last, after much wandering, and was rewarded with the view on the other side of the hill; rolling meadow-land dominated by a strip of azure sea, winking and shimmering against the skyline.

The most likely looking of the municipal-type buildings which stood in the square was one with the national flag pole above its double doors. Congratulating herself on her clever deduction, Janet made her way over, to discover that this was almost certainly the town hall.

It was, by this time, approaching four o'clock. Still no one stirred in the village. She strolled past a post box, and a shuttered front that looked like a tobacconist. The church clock said five to one. Obviously it had packed up again, she smiled to herself. Set in an ornate façade above cool dim archways and alcoves, the building was so brilliantly white it danced before the eyes against the deep blue of the sky.

She took her gaze on thankfully to the dark sombre doors of the town hall. They remained solidly locked, through to

42

five past, and then ten past four. Though she waited, keeping her gaze fixed on them in between impatient glances at her watch, they emitted not the whisper of a creak.

At twenty past four an old woman dressed entirely in black trudged across the square carrying a basketful of field herbs. A little later, a grizzled donkey hobbled by pulling a rickety square cart driven by a shrivelled brown man under a big hat.

Getting on for half past four, the doors to the town hall were mysteriously opened, Janet didn't see who it was who performed the miracle! She heard a rattling and a creaking from inside, but when she stepped through into the dimness there was nothing to be seen but a shadowy flight of stone steps winding upwards, and ahead through open glass doors, a courtyard drenched in greenery and steeped in the same phantom silence.

She mounted the stone staircase, a little of her confidence slipping away as the sound of her footsteps echoed away to the very roof of the building. Up on a very drab landing she was met by a very drab door, but the roughly painted sign hung lopsided over the letter box lifted her heart. *Ayuntamiento*.

She checked with her Spanish book just to make sure that it really did mean Town Hall, then, all her carefully rehearsed Spanish phrases at the ready, she went inside.

It was the smallest council room she was ever likely to see, being about ten feet by five. Alongside the door was a sombre wooden counter, and behind this stood an old green metal filing cabinet. The sole decoration on the putty-coloured walls was a faded commercial calendar hung opposite the door.

Janet addressed her opening remark to the man who stood leaning negligently against a high stool behind the counter flicking absently through a newspaper. He wore a thin grey uniform which had a wrinkled lived-in look about it. His face, showing traces of the afternoon siesta, was still

43

puffy with sleep.

'*Buenas tardes.*' Janet smiled at him uncertainly. '*Quiero audiencia con alcalde.*'

'*Qué?*' The clerk's face, blank before, grew even blanker as he looked at her.

Janet blushed madly. She knew her accent was bad, but she didn't think it was that bad. She tried again, reciting the words slowly so that they must have some meaning. The man, anxious to put her out of her misery, listened attentively. He nodded. His face brightened. It almost seemed as though he understood. Then looking blank again he winced apologetically, '*Como?*'

'The mayor! *Alcalde!*' Throwing all technical know-how to the wind, Janet took to driving it home by the sheer force of her words and her waving arms. 'I want to see the mayor. Me! *Alcalde?*'

At last a flicker of comprehension crossed the clerk's face. His features lit up slowly like sunshine travelling across a darkened courtyard, until he burst out joyfully, exploding with relief for them both, '*Ah, si! El Alcalde!*' He nodded vigorously and grinned happily, then his face dropped rapidly back into shadow again and shaking his head he told her precisely and quite definitely, 'No.'

Oh dear! Janet sighed. He obviously still didn't understand. She renewed her efforts and found that he did understand but she could make head nor tail of his reply. *Si*, he was happy for her to see the mayor. But no, it was *impossible* for her to see the mayor. He kept on firing the word 'Valencia' at her.

She battled on, and after ten minutes, and as many references to her Spanish book, she sorted it all out what he was trying to tell her. It seemed that the mayor was always glad to see anyone, but at the moment the mayor was in Valencia on a visit concerning council matters, and wouldn't be back for ten days.

'Ten days!' Janet wailed.

'*Mas o menos.*' More or less, shrugged the clerk expressively.

When Janet tried to find out if there wasn't someone else she could see on a matter which was of extreme importance, she was met again with that emphatic Spanish '*No.*' She must come back in ten days, she was told, and then she could state her case.

At a loss to know what would happen if a serious calamity befell the village while the mayor was away attending meetings in Valencia, Janet thanked the man with a wan smile and left.

She went down the stone steps and out into the sunshine with a feeling of anticlimax. Ten whole days! What a maddening waste of time. If only she had arrived a day earlier. Apparently the civic party had just left.

The Plaza de España was fast showing signs of life. The shutters had been opened at the tobacconists and children in checked smocks were skipping home from school. She went down the hill past shadowy figures in the doorways, cursing her luck, yet at the same time nursing a certain complacency. At least if *she* couldn't see the mayor of the village, neither could Mr High-and-Mighty Bruce Walbrook.

No sooner had she thought of the man than there he was swooshing round the corner at the bottom of the street, in a low-slung expensive-looking car of a lustrous midnight-blue colour. As he came whispering up the hill towards her Janet tossed him a flashing uncommunicative gaze. She saw by his gleam that he knew where she had been. She informed him in the same way that she knew where he was going, and walked on.

Reaching the spot where she had left the bicycle she found it surrounded by a group of children. They were chattering happily amongst themselves, but stopped abruptly when they saw her, fixing her with that same look of blank curiosity which she had encountered all the way through the village. She smiled to show that she didn't have another head tucked away somewhere and one by one they relaxed, some to shoot her their cheeky smiles, others to skip around.

They were obviously well aware of the tourist contingent on the island for as she pushed her bicycle out, they chanted at a safe distance, *'Inglesa! Inglesa!'*

Fascinated by their big black eyes and beautiful brown faces, Janet would have liked to get to know them better, but they were seized with agonising shyness and would do nothing when she spoke to them but dance or giggle at a distance.

Giving it up, she waved and started walking. The hill dropped away so steeply from the village she didn't trust herself to cycle down it until she had gained a little more practice.

She had arrived almost on to level road when she heard the whooshing sound coming down behind her, and knew without turning that it was Bruce Walbrook. She tried to communicate to him by the prim set of her shoulders her undisguised pleasure at his fruitless journey.

She was quite unprepared when he pulled up alongside her—so much so that the look of warlike satisfaction was still stamped on her face when she turned. It clashed with something similar in his own wintry blue gaze, then he was asking in icily polite tones, 'Do you want a lift back?'

'Thank you, but I've got my own transport,' Janet replied, straddling her bicycle haughtily, if somewhat wobbily. The dark polished car slid away and she was left swerving about the road trying to maintain her balance.

By the time she had got to pedalling along smoothly, the car was out of sight. She didn't see it again until she arrived hot and dusty, via the farm road, at the gates of the villa. Cycling nonchalantly past, she caught sight of the gleaming dark blue shape parked inside the gateway.

Round the corner, she wheeled the bicycle along the rough strip of track and left it leaning against the wall of the house on the terrace. There was no chance of sneaking indoors unnoticed with Dale around. He barked long and delightedly to let the whole world know that she had finally arrived back after her gruelling ride.

She found her mother fresh and vivacious-looking, after her siesta. Lucky enough to possess a reasonable figure, she wore new white slacks and a brilliantly patterned afternoon blouse, with a certain dated flair. She received the news about the mayor being absent from the village for almost two weeks with as much concern as if she had been told they had run out of bread at the baker's. And in her fussy comforting way she soothed Janet with, 'Never mind, dear, I'm just about to make some lemon tea. You'll find it very refreshing after your ride, and we can sit on the back terrace and let Dale have a run in the meadow.'

Janet went to wash the dust off with a frustrated smile. Later, sitting where basket-work chairs and table looked out over the low balustrade of the terrace, she had to admit it was pleasant and relaxing.

The sun had moved round to the back of the house, and mellowing slightly now with late afternoon it painted the outlines and ridges of the mountains with lilac and purple and pockets of gold. The countryside bathed in the same golden sheen was lit with a thousand colours that had never been there before; the bright copper red of the earth, the rich almost luminous greens of the trees and grass, the rosy pink glow of the villa walls, and the muted grey of the track.

It was fun to watch Dale's quivering tail and up-ended rear as he dug frantically in the meadow for the elusive fieldmouse, tearing off now and again to give the livestock at the bottom a stirring up. But afraid that she was enjoying herself, Janet said ruefully, sipping her lemon tea, 'This is all very well, Mother, but I didn't come out to Ibiza to sit and look at the view. I ought to be doing something about the track.'

'Now, Jan,' Mrs Kendall scolded lightly, 'it's no use tying yourself up in knots over something which can't be helped. You might as well relax now that you're here. And the change will do you good. You said yourself you didn't expect to get anything done in a hurry.'

Though Janet sighed, she didn't see what else she could do but fall in with her mother's suggestion. After her trip to the village this afternoon, no one knew better than she that nothing was going to divert the civic machine from its chosen course, not an earthquake nor a typhoon.

She knew her mother's routine well enough—pottering about the house and garden during the day, listening to the English radio in the evening while she knitted dainty garments for her grandchildren. After working and saving for more than a year, Janet didn't think that such a life would go down badly, for a while at least.

She sighed again, and agreed, smiling, 'I suppose you're right. Nothing will happen until the mayor gets back, so I might as well make the best of it.'

'Of course you must.' Mrs Kendall hovered happily over the table fiddling with this and that. 'I've got some shopping to do,' she sparkled animatedly. 'We'll go into town tomorrow and make an afternoon of it.' And on a pleased burst of affection she bent to give her daughter a quick hug, exclaiming bubblingly, 'Oh, I *do* love having you here!'

But though they had resigned themselves to the fact that there was nothing to be done about the track for the time being, Janet found it difficult to adopt her mother's equanimity during the evening when the cosiness of the indoors was disturbed by the searchlight glare of headlights swinging round the living room walls, and cars came, first one and then another, crunching up the drive to park with much slamming of doors.

On the pretext of stepping out for a breath of air, she stood fuming in the darkness at the sight of the big side entrance gates opposite, swung wide, and lights streaming

48

down the steps to welcome the noisy, laughing guests. Though the villa stood well back inside the grounds there was no mistaking that this too was brilliantly lit for the occasion.

Glowering at the high-handedness of the owners' calmly staking their claim to the track, on the advice no doubt of their precious lawyer, she flung her glance across to where the faint strains of music drifted out over the grounds.

She could imagine Bruce Walbrook blending in suavely with the party scene. The thought only spurred her on more, to get the better of him when she could.

CHAPTER FOUR

The bus to the town of Ibiza was supposed to leave the village at three o'clock. Mrs Kendall knew better than to be up at the top of the farm road before ten past, and the bus came trundling along at twenty past. All part of the Spanish way of doing things, Janet mused to herself humorously.

It was a perfect afternoon. The sun shone warmly from blue skies, giving one a feeling of delicious freedom at being able to go about lightly clad. Janet wore a dress which had a short-sleeved lemon top and brilliant white skirt with broad lemon band at the hem. Her mother was in patterned salmon pink with a shady hat to match.

The bus, like a fat red ladybird moving in from the distance, wheezed to a stop beside them. There was no one to open the door. Familiar with the routine, Mrs Kendall battled with the big knobbly handle and the door swung back, nearly knocking the two of them over. They boarded amidst her bright tinkling laughter and were met by a sea of passive dark faces.

The villagers were not apt to treat humour as a light matter. They measured out their smiles as possessively as a poor man counts out his coins, taking care not to let one go astray without first giving it careful consideration.

Unperturbed by the sombre scene, Mrs Kendall found two seats, nodding 'Buenas tardes,' in her bubbling way to the women of her acquaintance. She was rewarded with a glimmer of warmth in the dark faces and a casually muttered, 'Buenas.' But they couldn't forgive Janet for being a stranger and she was followed by their mercilessly curious stares.

The journey to town was made in a slightly hair-raising fashion. The bus tore along the country roads like a demon possessed screaming around bends on what was literally two wheels. Janet looked about her nervously, expecting to read similar lines of strain on the faces of the other passengers, but everyone was sitting so detached and content, even her mother, that she decided it must be only herself who was squeamish.

They arrived at last in the bustle of the Ibiza old town, at a time coinciding with the re-opening of the shops after the traditional siesta.

Mrs Kendall's shopping being mainly for food, Janet wandered leisurely with her through a lively fruit, vegetable, and fish market, and later around a modern supermarket which she had found some time ago tucked away in one of the side streets.

When all the items on her list were ticked off, Janet bought herself a good pair of sun-glasses and shady sun-hat. Being of practical mind she chose the latter in a creamy bleached straw so that it would match anything she wore. It had a tallish crown with a gay sprig of straw fruit at the side and a turned-down brim which framed her face and her auburn hair, she thought, in a not unpleasing way.

They browsed for a while amongst the pottery, carved wood, and chunky leather goods outside the shops, but being loaded down with groceries they were both in favour of making for a pretty square nearby where café tables and chairs in the leafy shade along the sidewalk had looked inviting.

It couldn't be said that the tourist season was in full swing, yet it was amazing the number of people, decked out in bright holiday garb, who lazed in the chairs. There were any number of cafés offering refreshment.

Coming in from a side street, mother and daughter stood considering delectably which one they would choose. It was Mrs Kendall who first spotted the familiar figure in a doorway across the square. In her gay, spontaneous way she called out as though she would catch his eye. 'Why, look who's over there! It's our lawyer friend from the villa. Now I wonder what he's doing down here?'

Janet had noticed Bruce Walbrook, briefcase in hand, amongst the passing people. As her mother spoke her attention became riveted on the building he was just leaving. It had the Spanish flagstaff outside and looked to be the equivalent, only more so, of the town hall in the village.

As the realisation struck her she grabbed her mother's arm and burst out with an angry gleam, 'I'll give you one guess! I'll bet you anything he's been to the town authorities about the track to see if he can go over the heads of the village council and save waiting for the mayor.'

She got the words out cursing inwardly at not having thought of that herself and urging her mother forward stepped out purposefully. 'Come on.'

'Where are we going, dear?' Mrs Kendall moved reluctantly under the pressure of her arm.

'If he can try it, so can we,' Janet said, hurrying along and keeping her eye on where Bruce Walbrook stood talking to another man outside the building.

'Oh dear, do we have to?' her mother complained, giving the café chairs a longing look. 'My feet ache, and I'm very dry.'

'We can have a drink when we come out. You're bound to know more Spanish than I do.' Janet, ushering her across the square, knew that Bruce Walbrook had seen them. She ignored that flinty gleam in his eye as he watched their approach, and before her mother could do anything but acknowledge the man with her bright eager smile, she dragged her past and up the steps inside the building.

The procedure was much the same as that which Janet had been through in the village council chambers. The only difference was that after seeing the clerk behind the counter, they were shown into an office where a man behind a

52

desk received them with a genial gold-toothed smile.

Janet made the verbal bullets for her mother to fire, but they fell from the older woman's lips amidst ripples of nervous laughter as she clutched at this and that Spanish phrase she had heard. What she couldn't put into words she mimed with about the same force that she waved the feather duster at home.

Perhaps because of a previous conversation, the Spanish official was familiar with the problem of the track. He was also adamant. He indicated with his own few words of English, plus several eloquently expressive gestures, that it was impossible for him to interfere in rural affairs. The disused railway line was the sole concern of the villages it passed through. If they wished to purchase a strip outside San Gabrielle then they would have to see the official of that village.

When Janet tried to tell him, with great impatience, how long the mayor would be away in Valencia, his shrug was typical of the Spanish disregard for time. He shook hands with them charmingly and walked to the door with them with a smile. Judging by his demeanour, ten days might have been no more than ten minutes.

As they went down the steps again all Mrs Kendall could talk about was that sit down and that cooling drink she had been waiting for. Janet accompanied her, engrossed in her own thoughts. If she had left her introspection until later she might have been more prepared for the scene outside. But too late—as they came out of the wide doorway she saw Bruce Walbrook and the man he had been talking to earlier occupying seats at a café table only a step away.

There was no time to avoid the attorney's blue glance. He watched her step out of the building, pink cheeks showing that she too had got nowhere with the official inside. It was his turn to glint ironically.

Mrs Kendall having already smiled brilliantly at him, and waved a hand gaily, he rose suavely, bringing his companion to his feet, and suggested, 'Would you care to join us?'

Janet would have liked to tell him coldly that they preferred to sit at some other table, thank you, but her mother, besotted at the sight of two urbane gentlemen bowing before her, pranced up and exclaimed delightedly, 'How very nice of you!'

Janet moved in unsmiling. They relieved themselves of their shopping bags, while Bruce Walbrook made the introductions.

'This is Francisco Cavanillas, a law associate of mine,' he told them.

Janet shook hands with a young man of about twenty-six or twenty-seven. Dressed in a pale coffee-coloured suit, he had a tall lithe figure and longish olive-skinned features. With his luminous, dark brown eyes and tightly waving glossy black hair he was breathtakingly handsome, yet his gentle smile indicated that he had none of the arrogant vanity that usually goes with such a face.

They were asked what they would like to drink, and Mrs Kendall chose, rather daringly, Campari with ice. Janet made do with a Coca-Cola. She had removed her sun-glasses while indoors. Now she felt an urgent need to search them out again. Not because of the sun's rays—it was just that they were useful to retire behind in Bruce Walbrook's presence. That wasn't to say that he was taking the slightest notice of her. His ear was tuned sympathetically to her mother's complaints on the business of shopping these days, and the high prices of food.

All the more opportunity to study him closely, Janet told herself, sipping her drink.

He was in a town suit of tropical summer fabric, exquisitely tailored, and pale blue in colour. The paler blue of his shirt exactly matched the ice-blue of his eyes and a royal blue tie gave his clean-shaven, sharply etched features a slight tanned look. It was impossible to guess at his age,

54

but he must be well over thirty to have arrived at his position in life, Janet decided.

She turned her attention to the young Spaniard beside her who was shyly trying to catch her eye. 'Have you been on the island long?' he asked, eager to make conversation. He spoke in cultured English with only a slight accent.

'No more than two days,' Janet smiled. She asked him in return, 'Do you live here?'

'Yes, I'm an Ibicenco,' he nodded, 'but I work on the mainland also.'

They chatted for a while. He told her a little about a law student's career, and the office he had worked in since he was twenty-three. Then Janet saw fit to drop a broad hint across the table to the effect that if they didn't hurry they would miss the only bus back to the village. Preparing to rise, she tried to drag her mother to her feet with her glance and her casual remark, 'It's quite a walk with all this shopping, so we'd better give ourselves plenty of time.'

She was rewarded by a vague movement from under the salmon pink hat, then Bruce Walbrook's crisp tones were informing her, 'There's no need for you to take the bus back to San Gabrielle. Francisco and I are leaving for the villa presently. We can give you a lift.'

Janet would have liked to stem her mother's obvious entrancement at this reply with a sharp kick under the table, but there was no opportunity. She had to watch her sink happily back into her chair, exclaiming on a ripple of girlish laughter, 'Oh yes, that would be so much nicer. And I haven't finished my Campari yet.'

There was nothing for it after that but to sit it out. At least Francisco was pleasant company. Janet paid no more attention to Bruce Walbrook.

When at last Mrs Kendall's glass was empty the men rose, Bruce Walbrook paid for the drinks and led the way to where his slim, polished car was parked in a nearby side street. He enquired if anyone preferred the hood up, but the air was warm and Mrs Kendall was plainly intrigued at the idea of an open ride. She simpered a little as the attorney suavely assisted her into the front seat beside him.

Janet sat with Francisco in the back. She soon found that her straw hat was a hazard in the breeze. Apart from that, she had to admit, the drive was an enjoyable one. The country roads were completely devoid of traffic and the sea caught in snatches was a wedge of deep blue amongst pine-clad hills.

Occasionally the car had to slow down for a strolling farm cart or a chugging tractor, but for the most part they cruised smoothly along. Janet could see her mother hatless and animated in the front seat, and as usual not short of something to talk about, although the buffeting breeze deadened the sound. Because of her amiable disposition Mrs Kendall had a naturalness that entertained. This was evident in the way Bruce Walbrook turned his glance her way from time to time, and with it on occasion the gleam of a white smile.

Though the ride itself was exhilarating, Janet wasn't sorry when the village of San Gabrielle showed itself on the hill up ahead and they were turning off and crunching along the farm road. The car didn't stop outside the villa. It continued on to the railway track and turning in cruised up between the two houses.

Mrs Kendall warbled her thanks in her laughing way as she was assisted out beside her own terrace.

Janet accepted Francisco's help out. He bowed to her mother correctly and kissed both their hands with the natural gallantry of his race, yet with a simplicity of style which was both pleasing and unaffected. Bruce Walbrook, dropping the car keys negligently into his pocket, turned and nodded courteously, 'Good afternoon to you both.'

'Good afternoon to *you!*' Mrs Kendall tripped off behind Janet with her share of the shopping. When they were round on their own patio she giggled amidst her parcels,

'What a charming man!'

'Mother!' Janet reproached her with exasperated disapproval. 'He *is* our arch-enemy.'

'I know, dear,' Mrs Kendall shrugged with a mischievous look, 'but he's still a very charming man.'

As soon as the front door was opened, Dale, who had been barking frantically at their arrival, rushed out and threw himself at the two of them before tearing to streak with wild abandon round the garden. Janet waited for him to calm down and fixed her gaze on the side entrance of the villa where the two men had just disappeared. She stroked the cat in the chair with a stormy look in her golden-brown eyes. Her mother might be dazzled by Bruce Walbrook's courteous charm, but he didn't fool *her* one bit.

For the next two days she saw no signs of activity along the track except for the lorry delivering her mother's *butano*. Then on an afternoon the most of which she had spent fiddling with the old sewing machine down in the shed, trying to get it to go, she caught sight of a figure leaving the house as she strolled back up the meadow.

She couldn't be sure from this distance, having only seen him once, but that tall lithe figure moving leisurely back to enter the side gates of the villa looked very much like Francisco Cavanillas.

On the alert she quickened her steps, her mind busy with conjecture on the reason for the visit. She didn't have to go inside the house, for her mother was arranging the tea cups on the back terrace as was her practice at this hour.

Janet strolled up, forcing a nonchalant air. She remarked lightly as she dropped into her chair, 'Did I see we had a caller just now?'

'Yes, it was that nice young lawyer we met in town the other day.' Mrs Kendall, in a flamboyant housecoat of fire-eating dragons on cream silk, fluttered over the tray like some exotic bird. She was obviously bursting with news.

Janet, knowing she would have to go and wash her hands, couldn't stir until she had heard what it was.

Mrs Kendall sliced the lemon and prattled in those tones of hers, spiced with intrigue, 'It's the Fords. They want us to go over there tomorrow afternoon. They say as neighbours we ought to get acquainted. Apparently they're having a few guests tomorrow and we're invited.'

Janet sat rigid as she listened. Her eyes flew to the high pink walls of the villa. *Go into the enemy camp?* The thought both fascinated and appalled her. She didn't see what good it would do meeting the Fords on their own ground. Yet she knew it would be both petty, and in a way, a sign of weakness if she and her mother refused.

Mrs Kendall was of the same opinion, though for slightly different reasons. She stirred the fragrantly scented tea in the pot, her mind on the invitation as she schemed excitedly, 'I must wear my blue damask. I hardly ever get a chance to give it an airing out here. There's only the British Residents' annual dance and then half the people turn up in beach wear.' She shot Janet a frolicsome gleam and confided, 'I must say I've always fancied a peek inside the villa, and it'll be fun to rub shoulders with the wealthy for a couple of hours.'

Though Janet was convinced that this was not at all the right attitude to take, there was nothing she could do about it. So the following afternoon found her in her room preparing for the visit.

She was determined not to make any kind of a splash over her appearance and chose deliberately a simple dress in pale lime-green, patterned with a white flower. It had a light ruffle at the elbows and a full skirt.

She applied the normal dusting of make-up, brushed her russet-brown hair so that it fell in its usual soft waves at each temple, and changing her bedroom mules for a pair of white sandals, she went to see how her mother was getting on.

Mrs Kendall was not only ready, she was itching to get over to the villa. Cars had been arriving for the past twenty minutes, she said. She was in such a state of agitation, they might have been missing the best seats at the theatre.

Janet glanced peremptorily though witheringly at the line of polished vehicles forming beyond the living-room windows. She explained patiently the wisdom of waiting until the gathering had warmed up a bit before putting in an appearance. She had to admit her mother looked at her best. The heavily embossed dress in lavender blue was perfect for her figure. The single string of pearls, and pearl drop ear-rings just the right touch.

A few minutes after three Janet gave a nod and they turned towards the outdoors. Dale, who had been padding miserably between the two rooms watching them get ready, slunk into his basket, his ears flat, his eyes big with hurt at being left again. Janet would have liked to give him an encouraging word, but she knew if she did, his ears would spring to attention, and his face alight with expectation, he would leap rapturously for the door, taking it for a reprieve.

Her mother locked the door behind them, dropping the key into her handbag, and together they crossed the terrace and the rocky width of the track, making for the side gates of the villa.

Janet noticed the cars lined up outside. Racy and expensive of continental design, one didn't need to look twice to know that these models were way out of reach of the ordinary motorist.

The big gates were open. They climbed the low flight of stone steps up into the grounds which were a mass of luxuriant greenery. Across an open square some distance away was the rear side of the villa; pink-walled with typical overhanging Spanish eaves to discourage the sun and tall white-painted shutters. Though a pair of heavy double doors were thrown wide plus several sets of french windows, showing glimpses of elegantly furnished interiors, much of the activity seemed to be round at the side of the house.

A white-coated waiter was just turning the corner with a tray of empty glasses balanced precariously on the raised palm of his hand.

'*Buenas tardes, señora, señorita.*' Smilingly he bowed them a greeting as though the tray were stuck to his hand, and waved them to where the sound of voices and laughter could be heard with that panache that only a Spanish waiter possesses.

Janet walked with her mother in the direction indicated. As they came round the side of the house, the first thing she noticed was the swimming pool. Its sparkling clear water tinted blue to match the sky, it curved to take in the side and the front of the house and was built down on a lower level. A fountain played in a separate section at one end, and gay sunbeds beside a heavy-fronded palm decorated the edge.

Up the steps from the pool two more majestic palms shaded the front terrace of the villa, and here, only a few yards away, three or four white-clothed tables, decked out with enormous sprays of flowers, held plates and dainty delicacies of food.

Of the people, Janet could see one or two down by the pool, daringly contemplating a dip; for though the April sun was hot the water was obviously cold. Several were lounging in the chairs and others stood talking in groups along the sides. The rest were scattered around the food tables, or strolling over the strips of green-lawned garden, to the right of the house.

It was all very informal, even Janet and her mother's introduction to the Fords. As they approached the tables, a heavily built man, smoking a cigar, rose from one of the chairs and the conversation in progress, and came forward to greet them heartily, 'Well, here's Mrs Kendall!' He pumped her hand, afterwards taking Janet's while he called around the gathering with gusto, 'Emmalina, come and meet your neighbours!'

A man inclined to corpulence, but showing little of it in his build, Ralph Ford wore his expensive mohair-silk suit with the same ease that he might wear a bathrobe. His angular, fleshy features were softened with a kindly look, though there was a decided shrewdness in the deep-set eyes. With his thinning, slightly greying hair he was probably just over fifty.

An arm around a shoulder of each of them, he took them to the tables and plied them with delicacies, at the same time offering them an infinite variety of drinks.

After a few moments Mrs Ford came hurrying up, having apparently extricated herself from some chatter elsewhere. A dark woman with good features, and probably several years younger than her husband, she wore a scintillating afternoon dress with the same casual air. She shook hands warmly with Mrs Kendall and then Janet, murmuring companiably as the four of them chatted, 'Well, this is very pleasant.' She was friendliness itself, but one had the feeling that though she would have liked to give you her full attention her mind was somewhat taken up with other matters.

Ralph Ford introduced the Kendalls around, in his friendly fashion, to the people near by. Janet couldn't keep track of all the names that were reeled off. She met a very tall man with crinkly waving fair hair, and another one of slighter build, with a high round forehead and a thick black moustache. A woman with a wide smile and a froth of chiffon at her throat took her hand, and two more sylph-like creatures in figure-moulding slacks and sun-tops gave her a carefree wave. Then the impressions became blurred and she just smiled around.

Her mother was already engaged in sprightly conversation with someone close by. Ralph Ford, drifting off with his wife to mingle with the rest of his guests, left Janet with the standing invitation, 'You must come over and use the pool any time you feel like it, Miss Kendall. José will always be on hand to serve you with a drink.'

Emmalina Ford gave her a warm genuine smile, and squeezed her hand to murmur, 'Do feel free to wander where you like. The house and grounds are yours.'

Janet thanked them and nibbled at her canapé. In the ten or fifteen minutes she and her mother had spent getting acquainted with the Fords, no one had mentioned the railway track.

She sipped leisurely at her drink, aware of the social atmosphere around the tables. She watched her mother, with her flow of lively conversation which nothing could discourage, twinkling with good-humoured affection. In her smart dress and pearl ear-rings she was just as much at home here as she was grubbing out the hen huts or potting a new geranium. It came to Janet with a smile that her mother was lucky enough to possess that chameleon-like disposition which enabled her to blend in happily with any kind of surroundings, whether it be joining in the social intercourse in the grounds of a millionaire's villa, or knitting woolly vests for her grandchildren in her own well-worn armchair. Janet knew also that this was the reason for her mother's unlined features and sunny disposition, and at heart she wouldn't have wanted her any different.

She finished her drink beside the table and wondered what to do next. She could see Francisco talking down by the pool, and remembering how pleasant he had seemed at the café table in town, she would have liked to go to him, but she was too shy to walk out across the terrace on her own.

She drifted instead past the porticoed front of the villa, with its patterned summer divans set back in the shadows, and wandered over to the strip of side lawn flanked by exotic greenery. This was the section of garden which ran past her mother's house, and alongside the track. But looking from here, the wall surrounding the villa was so far away with nothing at all to be seen above it except the blue of the sky, that she didn't wonder they heard little of the activity which went on inside the grounds.

Her glance was drawn towards a pair of open french windows showing a room at the side of the villa. With no one in the immediate vicinity she crossed the strip of paved terrace to take a peep. Seeing that she was disturbing no one, she stole inside.

The interior was cool and white and decorated with shell-carved alcoves, and leafy-patterned wall panels. There were silver candlesticks on pale polished wood tables against the wall, and elegant white ornaments graced various nooks and corners. The furniture was tasteful without being ostentatious.

Fascinated, Janet stepped softly across the polished tiles and made for an open archway that seemed to lead into a square hall. On her way through she was startled almost into a gasp to come upon a robed man-sized figure set back in the shadows. Breathing a sigh of relief on discovering that it was an inanimate object, she saw, on a closer inspection, a pair of slant eyes, and a mandarin-type moustache drooping around a secretive smile. On the head was a narrow-brimmed pompon hat. The outstretched arms held a large octagonal-shaped bowl used for—— Janet couldn't imagine what. To hold fruit perhaps? Though it was a little large for that. Or maybe to display a tropical plant? It was difficult to say. She was standing back, musing idly on what would look best in it, when a crisp voice came from behind her. 'The figure is terra-cotta, and it's early eighteenth-century French.'

Janet spun round to find Bruce Walbrook, a sheaf of letters in his hand, as though he had been in the act of passing by, standing a few feet away from her. She felt annoyed with him at creeping up on her like this. She told herself it was ridiculous to feel as though she had been

63

caught snooping when Mrs Ford had given her permission to wander where she liked. Yet that was exactly what she did feel, with those chilly blue eyes raking her.

Refusing to be cowed, she tilted her chin and told him, 'I was taking the opportunity of having a look round while I'm over here.' And her gaze travelled ahead to roam over a double-arched staircase, she added almost to herself, 'The villa is as lovely as I imagined it would be.'

He surprised her by commenting drily, 'You'd appreciate it more with someone to show you around.' He waved the sheaf of letters. 'If you can wait until I get rid of these, I'll take you myself.'

Janet, gathering the impression that she had no choice in the matter, watched him walk a few yards to where a marble-handled door was partly open. As he pushed his way inside, she caught a view of panelled walls and book-shelves, the glimpse of a littered desk and an armchair. Noticing his proprietorial air as he paused for a moment beside the desk, she mused to herself with carping disdain, so the great Mr Walbrook even had his own office!

She lowered her gaze when he returned to her. Though he was dressed casually in smooth sports top and pale slacks, she felt somehow stifled and awkward in his pres-ence. The villa was cool and silent, its thick walls shutting off all sounds of the outside. When he suggested that they start with the rooms around the hall she lied hurriedly that she had seen most of the inside of the house and was just planning to go into the grounds at the back. It was curious, but she found the air infinitely more breatheable once they were outside.

Bruce Walbrook escorted her across the tiled square and down a flight of steps to a path lined by evergreen hedges. As they walked they came upon dwarf palms, mimosas, rows of orange and lemon trees. Soon, however, one could do no more than rest one's eyes on the countless mingling shades of soothing colour; the silver green of olives, the rich emerald green of fan-shaped sunlit palms, the hot sultry green of the ficus, the cool pale green of bamboo shoots.

Wandering the paths of this lush paradise, Janet hadn't realised how relaxed she was until Bruce Walbrook suddenly spoke, nodding to a majestic growth. 'That's a mulberry. Gives a white fruit in the summer. Very sweet.' He pointed to a slim tree near by. 'This is a eucalyptus. With the high sheltered walls and constant sunshine it's possible to grow almost anything here.'

They walked on. It was strange, but now the pervading silence troubled her not at all. She listened as the man's vibrant tones brought items of interest to her notice; followed the blue gaze as it singled out something for her attention.

In the green stillness with the lean figure alongside her, she moved away from the paths, fingering fleshy tropical leaves, slender reed-like growths. In a shady spot numerous cacti were sending up spring shoots of colour. Enchanted by a bell-like cluster, Janet was bending to run her fingers through the waxy petals when Bruce Walbrook warned her sharply, 'Careful! There are hidden thorns there that can cause considerable pain.' He lowered himself and after a few moments came up with a stem containing a head of the bell-like clusters. 'Here,' he handed it to her lazily. 'You can examine it at your leisure.'

It had been Janet's intention to accept the flower with a polite 'thank you', then turn away, but somehow as she took the spray her gaze became entangled with his. Though it was only for a fleeting moment she had the feeling that those wintry, legally-calculating blue eyes, could if they wished soften to resemble a summer sky warmed by the sun.

They started to walk again. Something in that moment seemed to have lowered the barrier slightly between them. He said, guiding her round a spiky bush, 'You've met the Fords, I take it?'

65

'Yes.' Janet nodded. 'They seem to be very popular on the island.'

With professional dexterity he let her words hang just long enough, then said in his courtroom voice, 'You agree they have a case for wanting to purchase the track?'

Janet stopped for a second, caught off her guard. It didn't take her long, however, to get back into trim as she snapped, 'If you mean do I agree that plus all this,' she waved an arm, 'they should have the track too, while my mother has her strip of stubbly meadow with no entrance to it? No, I don't. I can't think of anything that would be more grossly unfair.'

'You're exaggerating the situation, of course,' he said testily. 'Your mother's house has every facility for incorporating an entrance in from the front.'

'I fail to see why she should do that when she bought a house with a drive,' Janet flashed.

'She bought a house,' Bruce Walbrook corrected in his maddening attorney's tones. 'The track is still an open question.'

'It wasn't until the Fords arrived,' Janet faced him spiritedly. 'Everyone round here was quite happy to regard the track as my mother's property.'

'Well, we don't work that way in the legal business, Miss Kendall,' he said, calmly taking her arm. 'As far as we're concerned, at the moment the strip of land is on the market.'

Confident that in law her mother stood the best chance of ownership, having lived beside the track for two years, whereas the Fords had only just arrived, Janet cooed, 'And as far as *I'm* concerned it's simply a matter of putting my mother's name on the deeds.'

Bruce Walbrook gave her his acrimonious smile and guided her back towards the house.

CHAPTER FIVE

As they ascended the steps up from the gardens, they were in time to notice Mrs Kendall with Francisco stepping out from one of the open french windows. Janet saw her mother turn and give her an animated wave. 'Ah, there you are!' she called. 'Francisco has been showing me around the villa. It's really most beautiful inside.'

Francisco came up and took Janet's hand in his gravely smiling way. 'You have been hiding yourself away from the party,' he said with mock severity.

Bruce Walbrook said drily, easing everyone forward, 'Perhaps we'd all better go and have a drink.'

Round at the tables, the knots of guests had changed about. Ralph Ford was down by the pool sat chatting comfortably in a little circle. His wife, though not on view, was probably engaged likewise in some other part of the grounds.

Janet stood by one of the silver trays while Francisco eagerly obtained for her the drink of her choice. He seemed less shy today. He told her he had been for a swim in the pool, but had found it a little cool. He said he went for a dip in the sea every day, even in the winter, and somehow sea water always seemed to be warmer than pool water.

Janet listened to him with a smile, enjoying his company, yet finding she was unable to keep a little of her attention from straying to where Bruce Walbrook stood talking pleasantly with her mother. She couldn't help noticing how relaxed he could look when it suited him. In his expensively cut slacks and smooth knitted top, he gave the impression of slimness, yet she knew by the touch of his hand on her arm in the garden just now that he had muscles of steel.

She had caught a glimpse before of that white even smile sloped on occasion at something her mother had said. She saw it now, and it seemed to her that the austere carved features were transformed by a lazy enigmatic humour that was oddly attractive.

Some time after five o'clock, the gathering started to break up. People drifted away to their cars, calling their goodbyes or waving a hand to one or the other of their hosts as they went.

Janet took advantage of this casual means of departure to round up her mother, who reluctantly bade farewell to the company she was thoroughly enjoying. After being escorted across the open square by the two men, they left by the side entrance.

Dale's excited bark at their approach could be heard above the thunder of car engines starting up along the track. Once they were inside the house he behaved as though they had been gone for two days instead of two hours. Mrs Kendall made a big fuss of him and crooned over him affectionately, but it was obvious that her mind was still over at the villa. Running her fingers up happily through her now somewhat dishevelled hair she chatted, 'What a lovely afternoon it's been. I really enjoyed meeting our neighbours. Didn't you, Jan?'

Janet gave the suggestion of a nod in agreement. Though it galled her to have to admit it, the Fords were really very likeable people.

'And their lawyers. Such nice men, the two of them,' Mrs Kendall mused, absently unscrewing the pearl earrings from her ears.

'Francisco Cavanillas is all right, I suppose,' Janet said guardedly, examining the cactus flower, limp now from being held so long in her hands.

'But so is Mr Walbrook too, dear, once you get to know him,' came the smiling reply.

Janet strolled thoughtfully to a vase of flowers near the

window. 'I wonder if he's got a wife in England?' she heard herself asking without knowing why.

'Not to my knowledge he hasn't. I suppose he's been too busy making his way in the world as a lawyer to think about marriage.' Mrs Kendall changed into her slippers with a sigh of pleasure. Then she gave her daughter a look. 'Why do you ask, dear?' she enquired, pausing coyly to add, 'I noticed you went walking in the grounds with him.'

Janet, knowing that she was being watched slyly as she put the cactus spray in water with the other flowers in the vase, to be revived, quickly turned away from the act. And at the pointed remark she snapped, 'Oh, Mother, don't be ridiculous!' Putting on a show of indignation, she ignored the teasing smile and flounced off to her room.

With still something like a week to go before any positive moves could be made towards securing the track, Janet was obliged to fall in with the leisurely life of the island. She would have taken over some of the chores around the house, but her mother had her own way of working, and she preferred to stick to her routine.

Knowing when it was wiser not to interfere, Janet settled for keeping her own room spotlessly clean and washing any items she found in the laundry basket along with her own bits and pieces. Most of the time she amused herself out of doors. Though the sun was warming up by the day the surrounding countryside still retained its fairy-tale emerald green look after the early spring rains.

The two enormous fig trees in the garden began to explode into a riot of shaggy green leaf. On the little square of patio the budding geraniums added a pretty touch of colour.

It was here that Janet got to know the various facets in the character of Twiggy the cat. As soon as the ball of fur heard a footstep she would drop down lightly from her chair and come forward for the affection which she regarded as her due. With still much of the kitten in her which made her leap into the air at odd moments to try and club a fly with a lethal paw, she could, when it pleased her, move with the deportment of a lady.

With her slant eyes and small features she had a bewitching personality. If you were inadvertent enough to stroll outside finishing a sandwich or nibbling on a biscuit, she would spring up and stretching her incredibly long arms would snatch the food out of your hand, swallow it down, then give you a calculating smile that dared you to scold her. If, bursting with annoyance, you were tempted to smack her anyway, she would roll over the moment you raised your hand, and, displaying her snowy white undersides, stretch herself before you in a siren-like pose of innocence.

Besides being a blatant thief, she was also a shameless bully. One of her favourite pastimes was to crouch in wait behind a bush in the garden, while Dale, all unsuspecting, wandered around sniffing idly. As he drew gradually nearer it was all she could do to contain the ecstasy of her excitement. She would fidget as though she was treading on hot coals. Then at the last moment she would spring out and land on his back, and as the startled dog galloped around the garden, she would hang on and bite his ear until he yelped with pain.

Sometimes to save her mother the job, Janet took Dale for a walk. She would follow the ribbon of path that wound down the centre of the meadow and then cut across the fields past vineyards and olive groves belonging to the farm. She had never known a cat who liked to go for a walk before, but Twiggy always insisted on accompanying them.

Dale, with a touch of the poodle in him, was something of an aristocrat. He disliked walking on prickly grass and stepped delicately over any rough patches. Twiggy was just a worker, employed to keep the mice away from the house. She knew it and she didn't care. Dale was never allowed outside the wire netting of the garden unless he was supervised, whereas *she* had the whole freedom of the countryside to roam in. And to prove it she would run growling with mock ferocity up the trees ahead of them.

Though they might be out for an hour or more the cat would stick faithfully with them. But her main delight came when they were returning to the house. Running ahead up the path through the meadow, she liked to sit down just a few yards in front of her victim. One could tell by the superior straightness of her back and her gently flicking tail that she was waiting with a wicked smile on her face.

Janet knew the game all too well. As the last footstep came down behind that lashing tail, the cat would whip round and throw herself, a mass of fur and four flying claws, at whatever part of the anatomy offered itself. If one happened to be wearing slacks the torture was bearable, but in a dress it paid to be ready to sidestep the hurtling ball of destruction.

Twiggy was a character in every sense of the word, and it was impossible not to love her, as Janet soon discovered.

She became aware too as the days drifted by that she was in danger of falling under the spell of this Mediterranean paradise. She welcomed each sunny morning; the endless blue skies topping the pine-clad mountains. With its clear light and solid colours, Ibiza, she was beginning to find, had a bewitching influence all of its own.

She kept an eye on the calendar and discovered that the day the mayor was due to return to the village fell on a Saturday. Obviously no work would be done on that day, so it meant waiting over the weekend.

On the Monday morning following, Janet rose and prepared herself once more to do battle. In cotton housecoat she ate breakfast with her mother on the little square of kitchen terrace facing the mountains. Mrs Kendall chatted gaily to her daughter about her trip to the village as though

71

she were going to pick up a few groceries instead of to wrangle over the lifeline to her house. Tolerant of her mother's desire to live a trouble-free existence, Janet kept a light-hearted outlook on the matter. When she had finished her second cup of coffee she went off to shower and change.

She chose a cream linen dress, which was neat and formal-looking, yet retained a dash of femininity. In straw hat and sun-glasses and sandals for comfort she called good-bye to her mother and pushed the bike out from the back terrace. She mounted at the end of the track but pedalled slowly so that she could sneak a look inside the villa gates as she passed. She saw, much to her satisfaction, that the dark blue polished car was still parked inside. From then on she was torn between the desire to pedal furiously and so get to the village first, and the need to take the trip steadily so that she could arrive for her interview with the mayor cool and poised and unflustered.

Once up on the main road, however, she soon discovered that the hot sunshine made it impossible to rush. Also the wheels of the bicycle spun the dust up on the asphalt surface, threatening to engulf her if she went at more than snail pace. And even then when she arrived at the bottom of the hill approaching the village, the gleaming metal frame of the machine was hidden under a thick layer of grey dust. She could only be thankful that she had escaped most of it herself.

She left the bicycle in the same place as before leaning against a wall, and taking her handbag from the basket she started to climb. A welcome sight half way up the street, or *calle* she mused, to give it its proper Spanish name, was a gargoyle fountain just off along one of the side turnings. Its head was set to mark a flight of steps down the hillside, and out of its mouth water spouted into a stone basin. Janet had missed it on her last trip, but she took advantage of spotting it now to soak her handkerchief and cool her wrists. She patted her temples and the nape of her neck and cleaned the dust from her sandals. Her handkerchief rinsed off again in the ice-cold water, she felt as fresh as when she had left the house.

The village was as deserted as it had been on her last visit, though lines of washing strung in odd places, and the garlic aroma of cooking suggested that there was much activity behind the scenes.

She crossed the Plaza de España, a little more life here because the grocer's shop was open also the tobacconists. Leaving these behind she stepped into the yawning black entrance of the town hall.

Upstairs she met the same uniformed clerk, who showed he remembered her by his friendly, *'Buenos dias, señorita.'* But then he waited with a questioning smile and she thought she was going to have to go through the whole performance again. However, a mere mention of the railway track and the mayor jogged his memory.

'Ah si! El alcalde.' He pointed to a building behind the church. *'Es en escuela.'*

Janet did a rapid back track in her mind over the paltry bit of Spanish she had picked up. *Escuela* . . . school? When she looked puzzled the clerk, trying to be illuminating explained expressively, *'La profesora!'*

Profesora? Teacher? *'Ah, si!'* Already Janet was lapsing into the idiom as it clicked home what the man meant. The mayor was the schoolteacher. She was turning to go when something else slithered into place. *La profesora?* Wasn't that the feminine? She turned back to the counter to query, *'Que es el nombre del alcalde?'* What is the name of the mayor?

'Nombre? Señora Casellas Garcia.'

Thanking the clerk, Janet went out and down the steps. She didn't know why it had never occurred to her before that the mayor might be a woman! Thinking about it, she stepped out into the sunshine and shrugged philosophically. Well, what difference did it make? The main thing was to get the track business sorted out. She made for the church and turned up the alley at the side. Halfway along she came upon a gap in a wall showing a large open space. New buildings stood over on the far side. She felt a little shy walking alone across the bare expanse in the sunny stillness.

To make sure she had come to the right place she asked a tiny figure in checked school smock, the roll collar coming up high under the small chin and buttoned at the back to protect every inch of personal clothing, '*Escuela?*'

The little girl, a thousand times more shy than she was, managed to get out a strangled '*Si*,' then she fled for her life. Over where a low flight of steps led up to open double doors, a few more six- and seven-year-olds were dotted around. The boys wore the same high-necked smocks as the girls and looked infinitely more mischievous in this angelic attire.

They were not as awestruck as the girls at the sight of the figure moving in. They leapt up and down the steps, and tore in and out of the doorway, eager to show off their capabilities to the visitor. Janet guessed that she must have arrived at break time.

Perhaps some of the children's excitement communicated itself to the teacher inside for at that moment she came to the door to look out. Mounting the few steps towards her, Janet got a quick impression of a woman of about forty years of age, attractive in a rounded kind of way. She asked pleasantly, 'Señora Garcia?'

'*Si*.' The plump cheeks dimpled into a smile.

It was possible that in her official capacity as mayor, Señora Garcia had heard about Janet's requests to buy the track, for she shook her hand warmly and led the way inside.

They skirted rows of small desks and forms and came to another larger room where separate tiny tables each with matching tiny chairs were scattered over the area of the floor. The children's dining room, no doubt, Janet told her-

74

self, noticing the cool whitewashed walls and ceiling, the dark-painted wooden rafters.

The mayor chose a table at random and drew out two chairs. While she was doing this, a group of giggling tots had crept in and were making a pretext of washing their hands at a wash basin against the wall. At the same time they darted cheeky glances across the room. A sharp word from the teacher put a stop to their giggles and they filed meekly out.

Settled in the low chair, Janet prepared to state her case. She hadn't been such a fool this time as to try and say it all in Spanish. Oh, no! She had used the time during the mayor's absence wisely, or so she thought, in putting everything down in writing that needed to be said. It had taken some doing with only her Spanish phrase book and her mother's dictionary, but she reckoned after filling a couple of exercise book pages that she had covered the subject pretty thoroughly.

She took out the sheets of paper now from her handbag and opening them out handed them to the mayor.

Señora Garcia obligingly began to read. Janet, because she had nothing else to do for the time being, studied the woman leisurely.

She was indeed attractive at close quarters. Her hair was dark and wavy and appeared to have been recently set. The pale tangerine openwork crocheted jumper she wore over a neat hip-clinging skirt gave a warm bloom to her dark skin and accentuated the rose pink of her cheeks; its short sleeves showed off to perfection her plump rounded arms.

She wore a gold wrist watch, the neat band of which sank into the flesh at her wrist attractively. On one plump hand flashed two expensive rings. A gold chain and pendant rested similarly in the curve of her ample bosom.

Occasionally, as she read, her sunny features were lit with humour. Possibly it was the Spanish she had written down which was a bit comical, Janet mused to herself. But what did that matter so long as the message was understood? This seemed to be the case, for at last the mayor placed the papers down and uttered a practical, '*Si.*'

Janet waited expectantly, hopefully. Perhaps the reply would be favourable.

If it was she learned nothing of it. Señora Garcia smoothed out the papers on the table while she framed in her mind what she was going to say. She took a breath, opened her mouth. After that Janet was lost, swept away on a torrent of Spanish that came tumbling about her ears, washing over her head, buffeting her on all sides.

As she struggled to stay afloat, gasping for the odd word to cling to, Señora Garcia, amidst the outpour, shrugged, lifted her hands, widened her eyes, traced her fingers along the table, and talked.

Eventually the torrent subsided. It became a stream and then a trickle, and at last the mayor brought herself to a stop and smiled.

Janet, dazed from the onrush, could only give a weak smile in return and murmur apologetically, 'I'm sorry, I—er—don't understand...'

The mayor gave her a puzzled twinkle, then as it dawned on her she rose. '*Ah! No comprende. Momentito.*' She called someone's name and after the sound of a scuffle a small girl came in from the next room. There was a rapid interchange of Spanish between pupil and teacher, after which the girl looked shyly on while Janet was told, 'Calle San Sebastian, *numero cuaranta y sies*...' The mayor wrote the address down for her, and made a painstaking explanation, the gist of which Janet couldn't fail to gather.

It seemed that the girl's brother Bartolomé worked as a receptionist at a hotel in town and had learned to speak quite good English. If Janet would go to his house and bring him to the school he would be able to explain what the mayor had been trying to say to her.

Janet thanked Señora Garcia, and smiling gratefully at

76

the little girl she went out. The paper said number forty-six, and she had been given to understand that the Calle San Sebastian was only in the next street to the school.

She went across the playground and out through the gap in the wall it would be handy to have an interpreter, she told herself, pleased with the idea. Save a lot of time and trouble. Pity her mother hadn't thought to tell her about Bartolomé, though she had so little contact with the village it was more than likely that she didn't even know of his existence.

Janet walked up by the church the way she had come and turned into the next *calle*. She soon saw by the low numbers on the doors that she would have been better to go along from the school and turn into the street at the other end. However, it was no good worrying about that now.

She checked off the numbers as she walked. Twelve ... fourteen ... sixteen. The Calle San Sebastian led out to the edge of the village and the houses became more spread out towards the end, standing in plots of countryside on their own.

Bartolomé's house turned out to be more of a farm and clung to the hillside overlooking the plain. Sacks of grain were piled up against the south wall, and two tethered dogs barked the place down, as Janet traversed the winding track. She came upon an open cobbled area fronting the house, where hens clucked about and potted plants grew luxuriantly green in the shade.

A woman in black, with black apron, was just coming out onto the step from the house. In her hand she held a saucepan. Flinging the contents across the patio, she eyed Janet with sharp curiosity and rattled off a question in Spanish.

'Bartolomé? *Vive aqui?*' Janet asked haltingly. The woman's answer was to shout across to the small building facing the house, 'Tollo!' She followed this with a tirade which was an onslaught on the ears, then turned back indoors.

Janet was left standing on the patio. In a moment a youthful figure came out of the outhouse, which was obviously the washhouse, for he was swathed in a towel which he was rubbing vigorously around his ears and dripping chin. He wore gumboots, and jeans zipped up at the front to hug his thin hips, and a cotton shirt tucked back from his soapy chest. He had a shock of unruly black hair, and thick dark sideburns which framed an impudent expression.

The towel coiled round his neck now, he gave Janet an unabashed smile which showed that one of his front teeth had been broken off halfway. This made him look even more boyishly mischievous, though he was probably eighteen or nineteen years old.

'Are you Bartolomé?' Janet asked, unable to help smiling at his infectious grin.

'Yes, I am Bartolomé, or Tollo, they call me,' he shrugged, his grin spreading wider.

Janet explained her business and asked him if he would agree to act as interpreter for her at the school.

'Of course. I have only to finish dressing.' His English was staid and musical and not at all in keeping with the exuberant vitality he radiated. In his clumping gumboots he swaggered noisily into the house, drawing Janet after him with the prosaic and grinning, 'Please come inside and take a seat.'

He waited long enough for her to enter a bare room, then trudged off further into the recesses of the house, yodelling at the top of his voice a snatch of some Spanish pop song. Janet stood around uncertainly, listening to the floating strains, and hoping he wouldn't be long. It was some time now since she had left the school. She knew, however, that it would be useless to point out that she was in a hurry, and in the end she looked round for a seat. The room had a bare stone floor and about halfway in at the side stood a small circular table draped with a heavy red cloth. Over this was suspended a bare electric light bulb. There was nothing else

78

then until the far wall where two wooden armchairs stood side by side next to a television in the corner and a sideboard-cum-bookshelf which was stuffed with papers and littered with ornaments.

Janet walked over and sat in one of the armchairs. Across from her on the other side of the outer door she now had a view of a yellow half-tiled kitchen. The light was on, and judging by the shadows on the wall and the clatter of utensils there was quite a bit of activity going on in there. Even now and again, while she sat and waited a woman, different from the first one she had seen outside, came into the kitchen doorway and fixed her with a sharp penetrating stare. Janet, by now, was quite used to the Ibicenco's curiosity and she knew no rudeness was intended by the stare. Just the same she couldn't find the nerve to smile at the dark set face.

She was beginning to grow impatient when Tollo finally breezed in through double doors at the back of the room. She couldn't think what had kept him. He still wore his great gumboots and he still wore his jeans. About the only thing he had changed was his sports shirt, and this he wore flapping about him and unbuttoned most of the way down from the neck

'Now I am ready,' he said grandly with his gappy grin, as though he had changed into white tie and tails. He led the way out, firing a barrage of Spanish into the kitchen as he passed which no doubt explained his errand.

On the step outside he stopped Janet. 'One moment, please,' and swaggered away out of sight. A second later she heard the rumble of a car engine, and then a chubby little seat, the model that many of the islanders used to get about, came bumping into view. This one had the dull look of old age and the interior was much broken down, but it seemed to suffer no other handicap.

Tollo got out to open the door for her with a proud air. She sat in on something which was more flock stuffing than seat, then he threw himself in at the wheel and tore down the winding track at breakneck speed.

Janet tried not to appear uneasy as they screeched out on to the Calle San Sebastian, shaved a dog sitting on the curb, and bumped and floundered round on to the street of the school. She hadn't the heart to look squeamish with Tollo jauntily gripping the wheel with his uncouth smile, and obviously showing off for her benefit. Twinkling at his unruly look, she couldn't for the life of her see him as a smooth receptionist behind some hotel desk, but she supposed in the right clothes he probably looked more the part.

He would have chattered on carelessly the whole of the way. Janet, however, considered it wiser to hold her tongue until they had come to a stop. Only when they had left the car and were walking across the playground back to the school did she feel sufficiently relaxed to start up the conversation again.

'Your English is marvellous, Tollo,' she told him smilingly.

'Oh,' he scuffed his steps alongside her with a modest grin, 'it is not so good. Every time, in the summer I learn plenty, but in the winter I forget it all again.'

Janet was about to make some laughing rejoinder when her eye caught sight of another entrance into the school grounds, probably the one the teachers used, over to the side of the main building. She hadn't noticed it before, but she saw it now all right, for parked just inside the gateway was a familiar dark blue polished car.

Her heart started to bang in her throat. She might have known Bruce Walbrook would be on the scene before long! She wondered how long he'd been here, and quickened her step, trying to keep the strain out of her smile as she listened to Tollo's easy chatter.

Inside, at the desks, the children must have been instructed to carry on with the lesson, for, apart from the odd stifled giggle, they were all huddled painstakingly over their books. Janet walked briskly past the desks, her eyes fixed on the open doorway of the children's dining room. Even before she reached it, she heard the resonant timbre of those familiar tones floating through to her. She went right up into the doorway hardly caring whether she ought to or not.

Bruce Walbrook was there, as she knew he would be. He sat opposite the mayor, and not in the least put out by the fact that his lean immaculately-suited frame looked slightly incongruous on the child's low chair.

That he had seen her, Janet was in no doubt. Still she made no attempt to back out. If he thought she was going to disappear on *his* account he was mistaken. After all, *she* had been here first. With this thought in mind she grimly stood her ground in the doorway. Tollo contented himself with slouching against the wall beside her, and sending surreptitious grins towards his small sister, who sat writhing sheepishly over her book.

Janet couldn't keep her attention away from the table in the dining room. She watched with intense irritation Bruce Walbrook's easy style and manner. It wasn't enough that he was looking his best, his pale suit enhancing his crisp dark hair and white smile, he was also speaking Spanish with the relaxed air and ease of a native. As he sat there charming the mayor out of her seat, she cheerfully hated him.

Señora Garcia, she knew, was totally oblivious to her presence. Her round attractive features were slightly flushed. She chattered, and laughed occasionally, lost to everything but the tall Englishman sitting across the table from her.

At last the conversation came to an end. Bruce Walbrook rose at the same time as the mayor. He shook her hand with a suave smile. She looked up at him with over-bright dark eyes and a certain coyness. She saw Janet and Tollo then and waved them in smilingly, showing absolutely no embarrassment at having enjoyed the company of their predecessor.

Bruce Walbrook greeted Janet with a slight bow as he passed her in the doorway on his way out. 'Good morning.' His blue eyes on her gleamed ironically. She looked daggers at him and left him to go in and sit down with Tollo.

When the three of them were settled around the table and in view of the fact that the Fords' attorney had already spoken for them, Janet decided to get Tollo to state each point of her case clearly and see how it went from there.

She stressed the importance, indeed the necessity of a drive up to her mother's house. She pointed out that her mother had lived beside that stretch of track for two years and no one, up till now, had questioned her right to it. She made it clear that the house had been bought on the agreement that the strip of track went with it.

To all this the mayor nodded gravely and understandingly, as Tollo explained it to her, '*Si! Si!*'

Janet felt quite heartened at her obvious sympathetic attitude. She waited eagerly for the replies. Tollo had to give these rather more thought, for the mayor tended to rattle on at length, leaving him no opening to make the translation. In the end he had to make the salient points as they came, lest he forget them in the barrage. He gave them to Janet, who was able to derive the rest from Señora Garcia's constantly changing expressions.

'*Si*. The *señora* understands the situation. Many people wish to buy parts of the old railway track where it adjoins their property ... the council have discussed this matter once before, but ...' here Tollo stopped to give the expressive shrug of the Spaniard, 'they have no authority to do anything about it.'

'But I thought it rested with the local villages?' Janet interrupted, swallowing her exasperation.

Tollo put this to the mayor, who replied with a similar deep shrug.

'She say,' the youth grinned, wrestling with the words to get the right meaning across, 'she is ... like this ...' He put his wrists together.

'Her hands are tied!' Janet gave the mayor a crestfallen look. 'But how are we going to get the track?'

To this Tollo interpreted the reply, 'She say she will have to write to Madrid to get permission to sell the land.'

Janet's heart which had been slowly sinking into the depths began to float up again. 'Can she do it soon?' she asked.

'*Si. Yo escribe hoy.*'

'She will write today,' Tollo interpreted.

Janet brightened. Well, that was something anyway. 'About how long will it take do you think?' she enquired.

The mayor hazarded a guess. '*Oh, un mes, mas o menos.*'

A month! Janet was horrified. But thinking it over, she supposed it was a reasonable time for letters to pass back and forth.

Señora Garcia rose, obviously feeling that she had left her young charges long enough, and Janet, not wishing to keep her from her work, rose and thanked her in Spanish for sparing the time for their talk.

'*De nada.*' The mayor shook her hand, in her warm, friendly fashion, and when she had exchanged a few light comments with Tollo, the two of them left.

Janet felt reasonably pleased with the interview. At least the mayor had shown herself to be sympathetic over the Kendalls' case, and she had offered to write to Madrid on their behalf. This meant that, despite the fact that she had spoken to Bruce Walbrook first, she was keeping an open mind on the matter.

Tollo left Janet in the *calle* outside the school grounds. 'Now I must go and get ready for work,' he told her with his slow broken-toothed grin.

She thanked him profusely for his help.

'Oh, it was nothing.' He scuffed about in his modest

83

clumsy way.

She watched him drop in, with a careless swagger, behind the wheel of the decrepit car, and waved to him as he tore round the block sending everything scattering in his path.

Turning, she made her way back towards the Plaza de España, then walked down the hill, with its magnificent views, to the road that led home. She got something of a jolt when she arrived at the bottom of the slope. Her mother's bicycle had gone. The grassy patch where she had left it sprouted yellow dog daises and waving green strands, but there was nothing to be seen of the red and chrome machine.

Worriedly she ran her eyes around the area. She was certain she had left it here against the wall. As she searched she moved up to the corner and let her glance swing round on to the main road. She saw the bicycle then. Caked with dust as she had left it, it was strapped to the rear of a familiar dark blue car which was parked in at the side of the road.

Bruce Walbrook was reclining behind the wheel pulling leisurely on a cigarette. He turned as Janet approached and said mildly, 'I took the liberty of stowing your conveyance in the back.'

Janet, beside the car, replied tartly, 'Did you have to? I find it rather useful.'

He leaned across, glinting at the way she had ignored his hint, and opening the door he said crisply, 'Get in. You're looking for trouble pushing a bike around in this heat.'

Janet stood her ground moodily. She didn't need him to tell her that. She had found the ride to the village very tiring in the hot sunshine. She hadn't been particularly looking forward to the journey back. Still, it irked her to have to give in to him. But what else could she do? He had made sure she couldn't cycle back.

Hating herself for lacking the strength to do anything

against his compelling manner, she slid meekly into the white leather seat and sat coldly upright while he pulled the door to across her.

The car whispered into motion. Janet felt the cool leather against her overheated skin. As they whoshed cruisingly along the road which seldom saw more than a farm cart, she had to admit that the luxury of the upholstery was like a cloud under her throbbing body. She hadn't realised how much the morning had taken out of her until now.

She was sorely tempted to drop back and give herself up to the sheer comfort of being transported home without effort. The only thing that stopped her was her acute awareness of Bruce Walbrook. He sat beside her, faultlessly attired, yet flicking the wheel effortlessly, one pale-suited arm resting over the side of the car. Also there was the fact that she had started off with a poker-straight back. She certainly couldn't continue in any other way now. However, she did go so far as to take off her sun-hat to let the breeze waft coolly around her throat, hoping he wouldn't notice.

He seemed in no hurry to get back to the villa. He took the car along as though they were following behind a stream of traffic, instead of having the whole road to themselves. Janet couldn't say she disliked the restfulness of the motion. There was time to notice the multi-coloured wild flowers starring the countryside around them; the startling clearness of the mountains. The breeze danced about the seats refreshingly. The almond trees looked too green to be true.

They came to the farm road. Bruce Walbrook turned in, skirting the huge carob tree, and for a moment they were drenched in its black shade. He cruised along down past the villa gates and swung in on to the track. As they crunched up its length, Janet smiled grimly to herself at the way he used the drive of *their* house as though it was his own.

She opened the door and got out as soon as the car stopped. The bicycle was unloaded and carried in on to the terrace at the same time that her mother came hurrying out of the house, a brilliant turban vying with her patterned cotton kaftan, flour up to her elbows. Undisguised pleasure was written all over her face as she gazed up at the distinguished figure. 'Why, it's Mr Walbrook!'

'I gave the bicycle a lift, and talked your daughter into accompanying it,' he said drily, placing the dusty machine down against the wall.

'How very good of you. Won't you stay and have a cooling drink for your trouble?'

Janet's frown was lost on her mother, who was fluttering her flour-tipped fingers and gaily playing the hostess. Bruce Walbrook paid no attention to her either. He gave her mother a slow white smile and replied, 'The idea sounds inviting.'

With set features Janet followed them both round on to the patio and stood by as the guest was offered a chair. Twiggy, the traitor, took to him straight away. She brushed around him, unashamedly begging for his advances, and nuzzled her snowy white neck over his lowered hand in a sickeningly affectionate way.

Dale, of course, considered him an old buddy. He waited for his pat, then settled himself down beside the chair as much as to say, women were all right but you couldn't beat a man for company.

Mrs Kendall, who had disappeared indoors, returned within minutes, minus her turban, her hair rapidly combed and set into place, and carrying a jug of fresh fruit juice, ice and glasses on a tray.

Janet found a place off to the side on a small stool. She watched Bruce Walbrook accept a glass, and as the tray hovered her way she shook her head. 'No, thanks. I'm not in the least bit thirsty,' she lied through parched lips.

Mrs Kendall helped herself to a glass and took the other chair. She knew enough not to spoil the peace of their surroundings by too much chatter. At the same time she was careful to balance this with a steady flow of pleasant remarks so as to maintain a relaxed air.

Bruce Walbrook couldn't have looked more at home. With the dog and cat at his feet, a glass in his hand, he chatted easily and smiled lazily. Once or twice Janet fancied she saw a flicker of amusement in the blue gaze that clashed with hers. She had an idea he was enjoying himself at her expense.

She sat it out, and pretended to be indifferent to his thoughts and his company. Yet when he wasn't looking at her, she found herself drawn towards his conversation; towards watching the way his smile sloped, and the way he moved his hands.

She surprised herself by experiencing a pang of regret when he rose at last to go. She watched him bid her mother a suave goodbye and hardly knowing why, accompanied him to the edge of the terrace.

'*Adios*, Miss Kendall.' He gave her a slight bow, before turning towards the villa, and taking out a cigarette from a gold case, he tapped it to add, 'As the subject of our animosity is now in the hands of Madrid, perhaps we ought to call a truce, if only a temporary one.'

Janet, with an odd lurch of her heart, couldn't be sure whether he was in a joking frame of mind or not. For herself, as she looked up into those blue eyes with their somewhat whimsical expression, she was certain of only one thing. The knowledge that the battle for the track was between them made her feel a whole lot safer at this moment.

CHAPTER SIX

MAY came, bringing with it a heat haze that shrouded the mountains so that they appeared to shimmer mystically in space. The lush green grass of the farm fields and country-side began to turn yellow. Tall swaying wild gladioli, rem-nants of the spring, still clung to shady spots and slopes. Here and there a proud cerise head could be seen above the waving corn. The swallows, a sure sign of the heat, darted and dipped and cruised close to the ground, carelessly dis-playing their poetry in flight.

Janet, feeling the need of sea breezes, began to explore the possibilities of going to the beach. She knew by the local map that the coast was only a few kilometres from the house. It occurred to her that as the railway had once been used to transport salt then the old track ought to be a direct route through to the sea. She asked her mother about this one afternoon when they were washing up after lunch.

'That's right, dear,' Mrs Kendall said above the clatter of the crockery. 'The old railway track takes you straight to the Playa del Mitx. It's quite a pretty little beach. I've walked it once or twice in the winter with Dale.'

'Can I do it on the bike, do you think?' Janet asked.

'I should think so. There's a well-trodden path along the side. It shouldn't take you more than half an hour, and I'm sure it would be much more pleasant than going by the road.'

Encouraged by her mother's reply, Janet finished the rest of the drying up, then hurried off to get ready. She put on a strapless swim suit, topping this with a beach dress which would allow the sun to tan her bare shoulders and arms as she pedalled. With a towel in her basket, plus her purse, in case she needed to buy a drink, she bade her mother good-bye and started out.

Dale was too sluggish in the drowsy afternoon warmth to bother giving her a send-off. Twiggy, game as ever, dropped down from her chair, skirted the garden and padded whisperingly alongside the wheels for a while until Janet gently shooed her back to the house.

The going was indeed pleasant. At the side of the track, which came from the inland direction up between the house and the villa and went on to skirt the hill of San Gabrielle and then on to the sea, there was a path of beaten earth which was smooth under the tyres of the bicycle.

It was true it was hot pedalling, but the various trees flanking the sides on different farming properties not only gave enough relief from the sun, but provided an exquisite setting for the journey.

There was the ubiquitous almond, apricot trees whose fruit was just beginning to show, pear trees weighted down with white blossom, and occasionally, as the track passed by some wayside farmhouse, the luxuriant greenery of a banana palm would cast its jagged fingers of shade across the path.

Sometimes the red rock-pitted earth would show up high at the sides where the track had been hewn out of a small hill. But for the most part it continued over even ground in an arrow-straight line towards its goal, the sea.

Janet was pleasantly surprised on her arrival. The beach was smaller than she expected. Caught in a horseshoe of gently sloping pine-clad hills, squat trees dotting its sandy slopes, it had an intimacy which would have been lost on an open stretch.

On the crescent of white sand there was a café kiosk and a striped canopied shaded area with tables, a row of changing cabins, and at the water's edge one or two white-painted pedal-floats rose and fell with the cool lapping of the waves.

Glad that she had made the effort, Janet slipped off her

dress and sandals in one of the changing cabins and paddled out for a swim. The experience was heavenly. The sea water had the soothing effect of cool silk on her hot skin. Along with half a dozen or more other bathers, she skimmed and splashed around for a while, floated to contemplate the azure blue of the sky, then paddled back to the shore to towel off.

It was pure luxury to spread her towel and lie out in the warmth. She had bought a bottle of sun-tan lotion and by the time her swim suit was dry she had acquired the beginnings of a golden tan. The pale peach of her sun-dress, with its splash of yellow flowers, seemed to accentuate the warm glow of her skin, she thought, combing her hair back before the mirror in the changing cabin.

She enjoyed a tall drink at one of the café tables and watched the antics of the May holidaymakers. There were one or two couples romping with their sturdy brown children. Most of the others were the Adonis-type men and girls, bronzed and self-assured and born to grace the beaches of these semi-tropical spots.

When she had finished her drink she gathered her things and prepared for the trip back, considering it wiser not to overdo it for the first day. The sun was strong and the glare off the sea quite fierce. However, there was no doubt that the trip had proved to be a practical journey, one she could make every day. It would be handy to come and take a dip whenever she felt like it. Another time she could bring a book and relax in some corner of her own.

The afternoon heat had passed its peak as she cycled back along the track. There was a velvety cool amongst the shadows of the greenery. The birds chirped in lazy contemplation of the scene, still too content to stir from their siesta perches. Janet pedalled leisurely, drinking in the tranquil beauty and feeling a little guilty at being here instead of earning her living amidst the boom and throb of London.

She corresponded regularly with Nona, her flatmate, who

made no secret of the fact that she envied her to distraction. However, Nona had this soft spot for the store manager by way of compensation, and reading between the lines the romance seemed to be blossoming.

Janet mused to herself on her friend's letters describing flat life, and the various ups and downs of Angela, the model, who had moved in for the summer. It all seemed worlds away from the life she was living here in Ibiza.

She had started out early, so that it was only a little after four when she arrived back at the house. She had visions of her mother fluttering about between the kitchen and the back terrace, preparing her favourite drink of lemon tea. Pushing the bike with a humorous light, Janet had no doubt that a second cup and saucer would be whisked out for her benefit.

These were her first thoughts as she approached the house, but coming round on to the patio she discovered a curious thing. The front door was closed. She had never known it thus through the day. It was usually kept open from morning until it grew dark at night, except on their weekly shopping visits to town when it was locked.

She turned the handle and went in. Dale seemed surprised to see her. He had been curled up and sound asleep in his basket and fell over himself yawning and yapping to get to her. He stayed long enough for her to make a fuss of him, then, stretching, returned to the comfort of his basket and the contemplation of his dreams.

Janet, laughing at his laziness, called around the house, and getting no reply went off to rinse and freshen up after her ride. Quite probably her mother was down the meadow somewhere, collecting the eggs or perhaps milking the goat. She had discovered a way to make delicious cheese from goat's milk and she liked to keep a good stock of this in the fridge.

Before the mirror in the bathroom Janet splashed her skin with cool water and applied a fresh touch of make-up, and pleased with the dusky attractiveness of her bare arms and shoulders in the sun-dress, after her sojourn on the beach, she went off to the kitchen. No doubt the lemon tea was in the process of being prepared, so she might as well see what she could do to help.

It was when she entered the spruce little cooking area, with its gay coloured wall tiles and gleaming utensils, that she began to wonder about the silence of the house. Everything here was tidied away just as they had left it after lunch. There was no afternoon tray set out, no tea cups, nor a sign that any had been in use. And come to think of it, if her mother had gone down the meadow, wouldn't she have taken Dale with her for the romp?

Briefly she checked all the rooms, and after closing the back door behind her, scanned the deserted meadow. A suspicion was beginning to form in her mind.

She hadn't missed the line of cars parked along the track when she returned from the beach, but because they were a source of irritation to her she had preferred to pretend they weren't there. Nor had she paid much attention to the fact that Twiggy was sitting up on the villa wall, for she had lately taken to frequenting the other side of the track on her wanderings.

Now Janet began to frown over the line of party cars. Her eyes travelled down the meadow, then back towards the side entrance to the villa. She wondered ... was it possible...? No sooner had the idea taken shape than she was marching purposefully across the track and up the villa steps. Set-faced, she stepped out across the square and turned down along the side of the villa to find a lively crowd scattered between the terrace and the area around the pool. Everything was going full swing.

Crossly, Janet scanned the groups around the tables, and sure enough there was her mother, resplendent in somewhat dated silk blouse and flared slacks, chatting happily away to anyone who cared to listen.

Trying to appear nonchalant, Janet made for the table and edging her way in as though she desired a drink, she managed after a while to make her presence known to her mother. But it was difficult to gain more than half her attention. Pretending to sip her drink next to her as she chatted, and catching her eye when she could, she remonstrated furiously under her breath, 'Mother! What are you doing over here?'

'Well, why not, dear?' came the bland whispered reply. 'The Fords told us to come over any time there was a party, and it's so nice to have a chat.'

'But one doesn't accept the hospitality of someone with whom one is engaged in a legal battle,' Janet expostulated softly.

'Oh, nonsense, dear! The Fords are perfectly nice people.' Mrs Kendall turned to laugh gaily at someone's joke, and Janet, sighing to herself, gave it up. She knew that her mother preferred to pretend that there was no wrangle over the track.

She was compelled to stand and sip her drink. Now that she was here there was nothing else she could do, though every mouthful choked her. It wasn't just her mother's capriciousness which irked her.

She had seen Bruce Walbrook the moment she had come on to the terrace, looking lean and masculine in white slacks and navy-blue shirt, a white polka-dot cravat knotted at his throat. Her insides had stirred in a peculiar way at the sight of him. She knew he had never taken his eyes off her since she had approached the table and only a few yards away now, obviously aware of her annoyance at her mother's enjoyment, his blue glance as it met hers was laced with ironic amusement.

Janet preferred to think it *was* only his look which irritated her, and not the fact that he was in the company of two very beautiful women who were hanging on to every word of his lazy conversation. One had straight, shoulder-length flaxen hair and a faultless figure encased in smooth lilac trousers and a matching sun-bra which looked as though it had been sprayed on. The other one, in a simple but exquisitely flattering beach dress, fluttered long curling lashes beneath an upsweep of luxuriant dark hair.

Janet wished she could swing away from that whimsical blue gaze, which kept fencing tauntingly with hers as it maddeningly took for granted the female adulation. She would have liked nothing better than to turn her back on him. But she would rather die than let him see that *she* cared, even if he was surrounded by a dozen beauties.

Admittedly it was painful to watch the way he smiled or inclined his dark head, when one or the other of the dazzling females spoke to him. In fact Janet was fast beginning to doubt whether she could keep herself from running miserably back to the house.

She was on the point of doing something idiotic like that when a hand touched her arm and she was turning to gaze up into the flushed handsome face of Francisco.

'Janet!' He pronounced her name Shanet, exclaiming a little breathlessly as though he had hurried to get to her. 'I didn't know *you* were here.'

He was wearing cream tailored sun-shorts and looked as though he had spent most of the afternoon in the pool. With his lithe sun-tanned frame, and damp hair curling close to his head, his good looks were quite stunning. Janet basked in the warmth of his smile. She derived a peculiar pleasure from playing tit for tat with that taunting blue gaze.

'Hello, Francisco!' she laughed up into his dark shining eyes. 'Actually I've only just arrived.'

'Please!' he begged with a hurt smile. 'Paco!' And at her puzzled twinkle he laughed, 'That is what my friends call me. In Spain, Paco is short for Francisco.'

'All right—Paco!' she shrugged gaily.

His brown gaze trailed over her golden shoulders and soft curving lips. With boyish impulsivness he took her hand and pleaded playfully, 'Come for a swim with me.'

'I don't think so, Paco,' she replied humorously, pleased to note that the blue glance had lost its mockery. 'I've only just come back from a strenuous trip to the beach.'

'You went to the beach? On your own?' He looked mildly surprised. And when she nodded, 'But how?'

'I cycled it,' she said simply.

'You went by bicycle!'

Janet was amused by his horrified tones. She was beginning to learn that the modern Spaniard was more car-conscious than any of the other races in Europe, and would drive on a trip of a few yards, rather than walk it.

'That is quite unbelievable.' He looked down at her, and his smile something of a rebuke he added, 'Promise me you will allow me to drive you, whenever you wish to go again.'

'I couldn't possibly trouble you, Paco,' she demurred laughingly. 'I might want to go every afternoon.'

'Then I will go every afternoon too,' Francisco replied doggedly. 'I am free from two o'clock until five each day. Please say you will allow me to escort you?'

Janet wasn't sure that this was what she wanted. She liked her own company, and she had enjoyed the peaceful ride this afternoon. On the other hand she was not unaware that a certain blue gaze was hardening over slightly as Francisco exercised his boyish charms on her, and enjoying her moment she nodded up to him sparklingly. 'All right, Paco! I'll be happy to let you take me.'

They chatted on after that about small time things such as the weather, and how the party was going, whilst they nibbled at the food that Francisco chose, and sipped at the drinks. Janet gave herself up completely to the role she was playing, at the same time radiating a genuine warmth towards Francisco for the attention he was giving her. She fully expected him to wander off after a while to some other group, but he stayed with her until the gathering began to show signs of breaking up.

She had lost sight of Bruce Walbrook. She had caught the suggestion of a satirical slant to his smile at one time as he watched her, then she had gone all out to ignore him. When she had sneaked a look in that direction a little later on to torment herself with the view of him beside his lovely companions, she found that he had disappeared and the fair ladies were chatting elsewhere.

She didn't see him again until Francisco was escorting her across the tiled square to the side entrance of the villa. While they were laughing together, heads down over Francisco's bare feet, she noticed out of the tail of her eye that her mother was being escorted from the party too. She could hear her lively chatter and Bruce Walbrook's suave replies.

As Francisco, without shoes, was unable to go any further than the top of the steps they stopped off to one side, and against an arbor of trailing yellow blossom which cascaded down from the wall, they stood and made arrangements for the following afternoon.

They were there a good ten minutes, in which time Janet knew that Bruce Walbrook had taken her mother over to the house. She had heard him return, passing them by briskly to cross the square and disappear inside the villa.

She said her goodbyes at last to Francisco and tripped down the steps, while he, turning to wave, pattered back over the tiles in his bare feet and out of sight.

Over at the house her mother was fussing around talking to Dale and preparing to change. Her animated features were slightly put out as she told Janet, 'I asked Mr Walbrook to stay for a while, when he brought me over, but he was very abrupt. He said something about having work to do and left almost at once.'

Janet pretended to give her attention to the cat who was brushing around asking for milk. After the events of the latter half of the afternoon, most of which she had spent taunting the man as he had taunted her, she felt too emotionally washed out to make any reply.

Francisco called for her just after two the following afternoon. Her mother was having a lie-down and the animals were stretched out in the shade, so she tiptoed out with her beach bag over her arm. The young Spaniard was looking colourfully handsome in linen slacks and brilliant beach shirt and despite the fact that she had been a little indifferent to the idea of his accompanying her to the beach, she couldn't help but catch her breath now at the sight of his smile and those classic olive-skinned features.

She didn't know why Bruce Walbrook had taken it into his head to park his car along the track today, but she saw it standing outside the side entrance to the villa as she moved out towards Francisco's chubby little brilliant orange model.

She had slipped on a brief silk-knitted top and oatmeal cotton slacks over her swim suit, and there was no mistaking the open appraisal in the brown eyes of her young escort as he gave her his customary bow. She shook his hand, then, the formalities over with, they relaxed laughingly. She was allowing him to assist her into her seat when she heard the door of the dark blue car slam. The next moment it was speeding past the windows and swerving tightly round the corner of the villa and out of sight.

Francisco was giving all his attention to settling Janet into what was obviously the pride of his possession, his brilliantly coloured little car. He relieved her of her beach bag and placed it on the back seat next to his own. Then donning a heavy pair of sun-glasses which enhanced his good looks, if that were possible, he climbed in behind the wheel and they were off.

Relaxing, Janet took off her sun-hat and tossed it on to the back seat. She kept her sun-glasses on to combat the glare of the road. There was no sign of the dark blue car as they turned the corner out of the farm road, and they went past the villa gates too fast for her to sneak a look back to see if it was inside.

They came up to the main road and turned towards the village. With an effort she put all thoughts of Bruce Walbrook out of her head.

It was a perfect afternoon. The sun shone from a cloudless blue sky, but there was enough breeze wafting through the windows of the little car to make driving a pleasure. The countryside was veiled in that afternoon stillness which is typical of Spain in the siesta period. The banks at the side of the road were peppered with tiny coloured flowers.

They bypassed San Gabrielle and followed the road leading to the sea. Francisco swung the wheel leisurely, taking his glance from the front occasionally to smile happily at Janet. As they sat perfectly in tune with each other's company, he asked as a casual means of passing the time, 'How is your Spanish progressing?'

'Very slow,' Janet said, grimacing. 'Some days I think I'm doing rather well, and others I find I'm making a complete donkey of myself.'

'No one worries about that,' he smiled. 'But you must mix with the people. It is the only way to learn.'

'That's just it!' Janet laughed. 'I make a point of going up to the village shop whenever Mother wants anything, but everything is so confusing. So many of your words are so alike.' She turned to him to tick off on her fingers. 'Take *huevos* and *Hueves*. Eggs and Thursday. If the hens haven't been laying and I go up to the shop I find I've asked for half a dozen Thursdays. And when we're working out what day of the week it is, I say "Ah yes, today is eggs!"'

Francisco threw back his head and gave a shout of laughter. Enjoying his mirth, Janet went on, 'It's the same with *nueve* and *nuevo*. Nine and new. The other day I talked to a woman in the village and told her, "I see you're wearing nine shoes!"'

'But what about your English language?' Francisco retaliated playfully. 'It is even more complicated.'

'You speak it very well,' Janet crowed, meeting his twinkling gaze.

'I had to live for one year in England to do that,' he replied, swinging the wheel.

Janet shrugged humorously. 'Well, as I've only been here about a month perhaps there's hope for me yet.'

The drive to the beach took but a short time. They arrived to find quite a few holidaymakers making the most of the pretty little cove. Francisco parked the car, and having his swim shorts on under his slacks, had changed in a flash. Janet went off to a cabin and joined him later in the sea.

He swam superbly, his long lithe body and his big shoulders slicing the water as silently as a fish. Janet hadn't his power and he was soon ahead of her, well out to sea. Unnerved after a while to find herself so far out of her depth, she struggled laughingly back in the direction of the shore, floundering hopelessly as he bore down on her with a menacing smile and splashed tauntingly around her. He caught her as she all but sank in the hilarity, and faces and hair streaming with water they kicked and laughed back to safer ground.

It was much more fun idling in the water than it was lying still in the sun, but eventually they had to content themselves with this in order to dry off their swim suits for the drive back.

They spread their towels on a spare patch of sand beside the café and Francisco brought tall drinks topped with slices of lemon. They lay in companionable silence, pulling on the straws lazily and watching the life on the beach until it was time to go.

Both glowing after the afternoon's activities, they were content to sit side by side in the car and let the warm breezes through the window waft over them until they arrived back at the villa, where Francisco, having work to do, bade her goodbye.

As her friendship with Francisco grew Janet learned, though only vaguely, that Bruce Walbrook had other clients on the island, besides the Fords. She got the impression that the two men worked between the villa and their offices in town.

She grew accustomed to seeing the young Spaniard's brilliant little car draw up outside the house every afternoon for their trip to the beach. Francisco adored swimming and as she quite enjoyed the sport herself it was good to have his company. They would breeze away just after two and not return until the last minute when Francisco would dash away from her laughingly and take the steps at the side entrance to the villa, two at a time.

They were pleasant hours they spent together at the cove, diving for pebbles beneath the clear water, racing one another to an outcrop of rocks, feeling the hot sand beneath their feet when, for fun, they joined in some beach game.

Whatever the activity Francisco was never from her side. With his big golden-brown physique, his handsome features and damp tightly waving hair, Janet knew she was the envy of most of the female population on the beach. And yet, though she joined in the fun with him, and was far from blind to the attractiveness of his smile, he was to her just someone pleasant to be with.

Sometimes when she was lying on her towel in the sun, she would smile to herself at her peculiarities. Was there any hope for her? How her girl friends in England would despair of her! Here she was with a man with whom they would gladly give a month's wages for just one date, yet she remained quite unstirred. For Francisco she felt nothing more than a warm companionableness, similar to what she might feel if she were with her brother Ian.

That might have been the reason for the success of their

friendship, because they were both so completely relaxed. They could laugh and talk, argue lightly and scold humorously, and usually when they rolled up to the villa in the car around five, they would tumble out bubbling over with high spirits, or chewing over the end of some lighthearted discussion.

Then one afternoon, after almost a fortnight of such hilarities, their outings together were brought to a sudden and abrupt halt.

Janet had been aware from the start of Bruce Walbrook's displeasure at their friendship. She didn't know what had got into her, but she had to admit that secretly she enjoyed making the most of Francisco's company for this fact alone.

She knew that on more than one occasion when they had returned from their jaunt to the beach, the attorney had been pacing the area at the top of the steps, waiting. She had heard those impatient footsteps and had pretended not to know they were there as she drifted leisurely out of the car. She couldn't explain it, except to say that it gave her a peculiar feeling of triumph to linger laughingly with Francisco at the foot of the steps, knowing that somewhere inside the gates that austere blue gaze was looking down on them narrowing disapprovingly.

She had grown so used to holding the scene in this way for as long as she liked that it came as a shock one day when directing her glance gaily inside the villa gates she came face to face with Bruce Walbrook.

He made his own way down the steps to the track and though there was still a few minutes to go before five o'clock, he spoke to the young Spaniard testily. 'I'd appreciate it if you could spare a little more time for your work, Francisco. I presume you wish to further your career in the practice of law, in which case I suggest that you devote more of your attention to legal matters, and less to sloping off over the countryside.' The steely voice sliced on, 'The Hamlyn papers are not on my desk. It might be an idea if you were to see what's happened to them.'

'*Si, señor.*' Though Francisco looked somewhat surprised at the senior man's obviously foul mood, he lowered his head penitently and hurried up the steps into the villa.

Janet found herself being icily ignored. At the same time she was conscious of a breathless tension in the air as, over her crazily pounding heart, she watched the smooth autocratic features working in an odd sort of way.

She didn't wait for Bruce Walbrook to turn his back on her to make for the steps. Taking the initiative, she swung away and stalked across the track to her mother's house.

CHAPTER SEVEN

JANET saw little of Francisco after that. Though sometimes she caught a glimpse of his little orange car inside the villa gates at the front she had an idea that he was doing most of his work at the offices in town.

She seethed at Bruce Walbrook and the power he wielded. Her tearful pent-up anger was such at times that she could hardly contain it. She liked to think it was because of the man's despotic attitude towards Francisco, but deep down inside she knew it was because she had been deprived of that jubilant feeling of satisfaction which she had derived from crossing him.

She longed for some development concerning the track. She couldn't wait to hear that her mother had been granted full possession of it. How she was going to delight in supervising the building of a wall across it at the meadow end, and watching a gate go up at the front. That would let the almighty Mr Walbrook know that this was one case he couldn't take for granted!

As soon as the month was up she made a special trip to the Ayuntamiento in the village of San Gabrielle to see if there was any news. She came away slightly exasperated after discovering that no one remembered anything about a track and she had had to go through all the performance of explaining again, only to be told that nothing had been heard.

She made herself wait another two weeks before going up again, when she was given the same reply. She refused to be alarmed when Juana, the woman from the village who cleaned at the villa, told her mother that these matters had been known to take years. She couldn't believe that absolutely nothing got done in Spain. Otherwise it would long ago have ceased to exist as a country.

She didn't know whether it was because of her repeated calls at the town hall that the mayor turned up one day at the house. She arrived driving herself in a newish fair-sized car of a rich mustard colour. She didn't come up the track but parked at the end of it on the farm road. Janet saw her first and went out. Her mother called out a greeting and waved from the door, then she retreated to the kitchen, preferring to busy herself with the preparations for lunch, rather than become involved in matters concerning the drive.

'*Buenos dias,*' Señora Garcia greeted Janet smilingly as she walked along the track. She was dressed simply but tastefully in a slim black skirt which flattered her plump hips, and a frilled white blouse. Her round cheeks had that attractive warm bloom on them and her dark eyes completed a very pleasing picture.

'*Buenos dias, señora,*' Janet returned the greeting as she walked to meet her. For some time she was a little puzzled as to the reason for the visit. The mayor stood and looked around her smilingly. She admired the house and Janet's mother's ideas around the garden. She patted Dale who had ventured out of bounds along the track to make himself known. She gazed at the mountains, and at the farm on the hill.

When it seemed that the visit was no more than a social call she crossed the width of the track. She trained her eye down the length of it to the bottom of the meadow, then slapped the villa wall with her hand. '*Esto?*' she asked.

Janet's heart leapt. She realised she was being asked how much width-wise of the track did they want to buy. In the few words of Spanish she had picked up she asked if it were indeed possible to buy right up to the wall.

'*Si.*' The mayor pursed her lips and gave an emphatic

nod, slapping the pink-painted area again. She went on to explain with much gesturing that the wide strips of soil on either side of the track belonged to the government and anyone who wished could include the whole of this width in their purchase.

Janet wasted no time in making it clear that that was how they wanted it, and to give emphasis to her own gestures she also slapped the villa wall. In doing so, she experienced an inner feeling of elation. To own the last inch of land at this side! That would give Bruce Walbrook something to swallow.

Señora Garcia, satisfied with the situation, was inclined to drift off again. Her attention wandered towards the leafy almond trees across the farm road, as though she seldom got a chance to enjoy the countryside.

Janet tried to pin her down to something definite concerning the track. She pointed out that it was April when the letter had been sent to Madrid, and that two months was much time.

'*Mucho tiempo? No!*' Señora Garcia's unconvinced expression was such that two months might have been no more than passing moments in a summer's day.

Janet resisted the temptation to mention that originally the waiting time had been put at *one* month. She asked again how long it was likely to be before the Ayuntamiento heard something.

'*No se*',' Señora Garcia shrugged, smiling, and turned to go.

Janet had to be content with that. If the mayor of the village didn't know, certainly no one else would. It looked as though all one could do was wait.

She waved to the older woman and left her making for her car. As she returned to the patio, she had a slightly let-down feeling. She suspected now that the mayor had come simply to show that she was concerned about the track, but once she had left there was no doubt she would forget all

105

about it again.

Dropping into a chair on the patio, she looked up, expecting to find that the mustard-coloured car had gone. But it was still there blocking the entrance to the drive and beside it was the familiar dark blue polished one which had evidently been prevented from turning in.

And that was how it *should* be, Janet told herself with an acid gleam of complacency.

She was in time to see Bruce Walbrook stepping out lazily from the driving seat. He greeted the mayor with that suave charm of his. Señora Garcia acknowledged him with a coy vivaciousness.

Head down, Janet pretended to fondle Twiggy the cat on her knee as she listened to the pleasant interchange in rapid Spanish. It irritated her when it went on and on. She couldn't imagine what Señora Garcia was finding to talk about for so long. Her laughter, though musical, stretched Janet's nerves until she thought they would snap.

From time to time she stole a look at the lean masculine figure beside the mayor. Even from this distance she recognised the superb cut of the straw-coloured tropical summer suit. Dark sun-glasses heightened the tan of the lean features and the whiteness of that slow-forming smile.

Twiggy, playful as ever, was at her most vicious just now, probably because Janet gripped her tighter than she had intended to at times. She kept her head down, absently avoiding the cat's razor-sharp claws, while her whole body stayed tautly tuned to the activity at the end of the track.

She heard the car doors slam at last and jumped up, anxious to disappear indoors before Bruce Walbrook came up the drive. She knew he would look towards the house as he drove past. He always did these days. And Janet always made a point of not being on view. Though when he had gone by, she would invariably wander to the curtained window in the living room and watch him get out at the side gates of the villa.

As her mother clattered busily in the kitchen she watched him now, stepping out with his briefcase in his hand. She was careful to keep out of sight as his glance strayed towards the house. He took the steps effortlessly, his slim figure erect. Janet watched him until he disappeared from view, then she turned abruptly away. She wondered why her heart felt weighted down, like lead. She supposed that it must be that although the mayor had put in an appearance at the house today, they were still no nearer to owning the track.

The heat became less bearable as the days passed. Janet had watched June come in, painting the lifeless-looking creepers that trailed down the villa walls in a riot of colour. A deep, rich red bougainvillaea showered its blossom now over the side entrance, and touches of cool whites, delicate pinks, and flaming orange caught the eye down the length of the track.

With July the countryside wilted. There was nothing to be seen of the rich green fields of spring. The grass lay stunted and burnt close to the ground which was hard and cracked. The sky, pale and washed out, pulsed with heat projecting the mountains as molten blurs of shape in the pearly haze.

And yet there was a subtle attractiveness about the scorched land, a primitive beauty in the violent reds and browns of the stark earth; in the dusty, ragged look of the almond trees heavy with fruit and the white village of San Gabrielle on the hillside, throbbing under the sun. About it all there was a kind of brooding enchantment that stirred the senses in an odd way.

But though the countryside decayed in the heat, the villa gardens flourished. Down at the meadow end looking across the track Janet caught glimpses of exotic flowering trees and shiny tropical leaves. She longed to walk along the paths beyond those walls, amongst the cool green of the palms and beneath the shady bowers. She knew no one would mind if she entered the side gates and descending the steps from the square, wandered leisurely at her will. But her pride kept her from going over there.

For the same reason she continued to cycle to the beach on her own every afternoon. With the peak of the summer the number of guests arriving at the villa had increased and there was a new vivacity amongst the crowd. Flamboyant continental types, ebullient Scandinavians, they came speeding down the track on party afternoons, laughing loudly as they alighted from their cars.

Janet refused to stay around and endure the gaiety. Though it was something of a gruelling trip now cycling to the beach in the heat, she preferred it to hanging about the house. The sight of tall ravishing females drifting towards the villa gates where the dark blue polished car was parked gave her a sick feeling in the pit of her stomach, and as soon as she could she packed her beach bag and left.

She knew that her mother tripped over to rub shoulders with the smart set around the pool while she was away. Sometimes when she arrived home a little early after her swim, she would find the front door closed and the lingerings of her heavy violet perfume on the air. But it was useless to talk about it. Her mother was dazzled by the glamour of it all and saw nothing wrong in enjoying herself over at the villa whenever she could.

This knowledge made the going all the harder for Janet on her lone trudges to the beach. She was beginning to feel that she was fighting a one-woman battle against the villa.

Then one afternoon when she returned from the beach to the sounds of a party in full swing over at the villa she was mildly surprised to find her mother at home.

It was a heavy oppressive day with thick cloud and not a flicker of breeze to disperse the heat. Janet had splashed around for a little while at the cove, then changing into strapless sun-dress and sandals she had pedalled back slowly to stay cool.

The track, when she arrived home, was choked with expensive cars, and laughter and music could be heard drifting out over the villa walls. She entered the house expecting to find it empty, but her mother was in the living room. She was sitting in her armchair weeping softly.

'Why, Mother!' Janet dropped her beach bag and hurried over to her. 'What's wrong?'

Mrs Kendall dabbed at her eyes with her handkerchief. 'It's Twiggy,' she said in between sniffles.

'Well, what's the matter with her?' Janet asked, kneeling.

'She's dead,' came the muffled reply.

'*Dead?*' Janet went cold with shock. 'How can she be?'

'I was going over to join the party.' Mrs Kendall blew her nose. 'I saw her. She's lying on the track. She must have been hit by one of the cars.'

On a wave of white-hot anger Janet rose and rushed out. She stumbled across the track, her horrified gaze raking the ground. Only this morning she had seen Twiggy prancing along here, darting after imaginary flies.

She found her at last, a little to one side of the steps. She was lying stiffly with her paws stretched out. Her mouth was slightly open, showing her tiny pointed teeth. As Janet gazed on her a surge of hot tears rushed to her eyes. She turned wildly towards the villa gates. Someone was going to pay for this!

She mounted the steps and crossed the square through a blinding red mist. She was oblivious to the noise and uproarious laughter coming from the terrace. Her only concern when she turned the corner of the villa was knowing the whereabouts of Mr and Mrs Ford.

It was only to be expected that she wouldn't see any sign of them amidst the whirl of people circulating around the tables and the pool. But that wouldn't stop her, she told herself through her tears. She would search them out wherever they were.

She was just about to storm in when Bruce Walbrook, standing glass in hand, alone, on the edge of the gathering, spotted her. His glance taking in her white contorted features and brimming gaze, he moved swiftly towards her. Before anyone had time to notice her he had taken her by the arm and turning her away with him, asked softly under his breath, 'Is anything wrong?'

Janet had been about to let fly with all manner of things. Now suddenly she found, with his touch on her arm, that she could do nothing but close her eyes over the dazzle of tears.

'In here.' The hand dropped across her shoulders and she was led through an open door near by into the villa. In the cool interior she felt herself being guided along until they arrived at the small study she had caught a glimpse of on her last visit.

Bruce Walbrook opened the door of the mellow book-lined room and drawing her inside closed it again after them.

'Now,' his blue gaze searched her face, 'what's the trouble?'

Janet had recovered some of her composure by this time and with it her anger returned twofold. She saw now the discreet manner in which he had got her out of the way and so prevented her from making a scene in the villa grounds.

'It's Twiggy,' she blazed out. She caught the flicker of incomprehension that passed across his face and flung at him, 'Our cat. She's been killed by one of the villa's mad cars. She's lying on the track ... My mother saw her when she was coming over here ... It's only what I expected ...' She struggled to hold back the tears, but the flood was too great and collapsing incoherently she sank sobbing into the chair.

Past caring now, she gave herself up completely to her misery. It wasn't just this afternoon's blow. The whole

110

wretched business of the track and her fight with the villa had worn her down until at the moment she didn't care whether she fought or not.

She didn't know how long she had been sitting there giving way to her tears, when Bruce Walbrook placed a glass containing amber liquid on the desk beside her with the order, 'Drink it. You'll feel better.'

'I don't want it.' She shook her head vigorously.

'Do as I say.' Firmly he turned her fingers round the glass. 'Sip it slowly. I'll be back in a few moments.'

She heard him close the door softly behind him as he went out. Because it was in her hand she took a sip of the liquid in the glass. It tasted vile, but after a few moments she felt its steadying effect on her racked body. Realising that she had made a complete fool of herself, she was at pains now to present a cold, calm exterior. Little by little she took the full contents of the glass.

She had dried her eyes and tidied her hair, and except for the sorrow behind her gaze when she thought of poor Twiggy's end, she was sitting quiet and composed when Bruce Walbrook returned.

The immaculate cuffs of his white shirt were rolled back as though he had just been washing his hands. As he turned them down and fastened them with heavy cuff links Janet caught his gaze and she knew then what he had been outside to do.

She blinked back a fresh blur of tears and said jerkily, 'I'd better be getting home.'

'I'll walk to the gate with you.' He opened the door.

'You don't have to,' she replied dry-eyed again, 'I'm perfectly all right.'

He took her arm as though he hadn't heard and accompanied her through the shadowy interior, and out across the open square to the steps. The grip of his fingers was firm on her arm as they went down the flight together.

Though she tried not to look, Janet found her gaze drawn

111

to that spot at the side of the gate. There was nothing there now except a speck of blood on the ground.

Wordlessly she broke free of the grip on her arm and hurried across to the house.

CHAPTER EIGHT

SUMMER was at its zenith. The island was crowded with holidaymakers. Sometimes the sightseeing coaches could be heard going along the main highway beyond the farm road. The villa stood somnolent in the heat, apparently lifeless except on social afternoons.

Janet spent the days drifting about the meadow listening to the heavy silence that shrouded the countryside. She couldn't help seeing Twiggy prancing down the path ahead of her when she walked. She seemed to see her little calculating face and flying white paws no matter where she put her tear-starred gaze.

She knew she was being foolish. No one else gave Twiggy a thought. She was just a cat who had unfortunately been run over. Janet's mother had soon forgotten the episode. Janet could easily get another kitten from the farm, and she had Dale.

Though she tried to think of other things, each day Janet found herself drawn towards the patch of disturbed soil which she had discovered at the base of the big almond tree, down at the bottom of the meadow. Standing here gazing out beyond the greenery she seemed to feel an answering sadness in the breeze that rustled over the countryside.

She was mooning here one afternoon when the harsh sound of footsteps approaching over the rough surface of the track dragged her back from her melancholy wanderings. She turned to see Francisco hobbling his way over the rocky pebbles towards her. '*Holà!*' he greeted her in Spanish.

'Hello,' she smiled wanly. Since he had been assigned to

doing most of his work at the offices in town she had seen little of him over the past few weeks.

'I have come to tell you that we are going for a drive.' He walked across to join her on the soft faded grass. In the green shade his handsome good looks were warmed by his friendly smile. He was casually but tastefully attired in patterned beach shirt and linen slacks.

Janet lacked the spark to make any kind of a reply, and he went on, 'We are to be a foursome. You and your mother, and Bruce and I. Come, you must get ready.' He took her by the arm and urged her along the path.

Janet let him guide her up the meadow simply because she had no willpower to refuse. She suspected that Bruce had sent him, and that the outing was his idea. She had sensed him watching her from within the villa grounds at the side entrance, most days as she wandered about at the foot of the almond tree, but she had felt too forlorn to care about his presence.

In the house when she arrived her mother was flying about full of fuss and animation. 'Isn't it heavenly? Bruce is taking us all for a drive!' Her fingers trembling with delight as she removed the rollers from her turbanned hair. Dropping them in a trail over the furniture as she hurried to her bedroom, she warbled, 'I shall wear my green chiffon.'

Following her in her blouse and slacks, Janet gave a lacklustre shrug. 'I'll just wash my face.'

'Oh, put on something pretty, dear.' Mrs Kendall turned back to show her disappointment at the remark. Never one to miss the chance of making a show, she coaxed gaily, 'We must do the men justice, you know!'

To please her mother, Janet fingered lethargically through her wardrobe in her bedroom. She unhooked a white nylon dress that she hadn't worn yet during her stay, because it was a little too grand for the countryside and their shopping visits to town. But it was probably suitable for an afternoon drive, she supposed, tossing it on to the bed.

Strangely enough, when she had showered briefly, brushed on a light skin perfume and slipped into the appropriate underwear, she felt a slight lifting of her spirits as she fastened up the tiny pearl-drop buttons at the front of the bodice.

The dress had a neat round collar and small cap sleeves and the skirt was a swirl of sunray pleats over a filmy underslip. Her face, russet-gold from the sun, needed nothing but a touch of peach-tinted lipstick. She smoothed up her hair into its usual style with a brush and sorting out a straw handbag to go with her sun-hat and white low-heeled sandals, considered she had done her best.

She got something of a shock when she went through into the living room and found Bruce waiting there. Lean and tanned and dressed with his usual polish in royal blue slacks and pale blue tailored beach jacket, he looked heart-joltingly incongruous amongst her mother's somewhat dated bric-à-brac. There was time only for her glance to come up against his, then her mother was sweeping through behind her, a vision in her green chiffon, and floppy green hat, a long link of amber beads on her chest.

Bruce Walbrook stooped to meet her amidst the cluttered confines of the room and turned towards the door with a lazy, 'Are we all set?'

Janet threw a look of concern down at Dale. He was dodging people's feet, his ears going up and down because of all the fuss. His eyes, which were glazing over with misery at the thought of being left, still showed a light of hope.

Bruce, following Janet's glance, took in the sight of him. His blue gaze lapsing whimsical, he snapped his fingers to drawl, 'All right, old chap. You might as well come along too.'

Dale didn't wait to be asked twice. Before anyone could change their minds he threw himself outside and jumping and turning, led the way with his excited barks. Mrs Kendall, revelling in all the noise and fuss, fluttered out laughingly along with him towards the cars.

Janet saw Francisco standing smilingly beside his little orange machine. Without giving it much thought she drifted towards him. At the same time Bruce assisted her mother into the seat of his dark blue conveyance, closing the door as Dale helped himself to a place on her lap.

With everyone settled, the two cars started out, the dark blue one in the lead. They crunched slowly up the farm road and out on to the main highway. From here they took the road to the coast.

Cruising along in Francisco's restful presence, the breeze rustling in at the open windows, Janet couldn't stir herself to react much to the scenery. And yet, as she watched the polished car a little in front of them, and saw that dark head of hair and those pale blue-clad shoulders alongside the green blob of her mother's hat, there was, piercing the inner mists of her lethargy, the glimmerings of a golden feeling which told her there was something special about the day.

The sea, when they arrived, was a strip of azure blue pasted against the skyline, coins of gold glinting and flashing across its middle where the sun struck it.

On the coast road they drove south to take in the Playa Es Cana. The route led through a lovely stretch of country. The red earth was planted with olive trees, later giving way to pinewoods that opened on to the beautiful bay of Es Cana. They circled the small peninsula, passing a large hotel and a holiday village, then continued on towards Santa Eulalia.

This was a sleepy, unsophisticated little spot with a green square encircled by pleasant bars and shadowed by palm trees. Along its main street, colourful boutiques and souvenir shops mingled with grocery shops and general stores. It was a pretty but cluttered little town and they were soon leaving it behind and making for Ibiza.

They skirted the city with its cathedral and arched and balconied houses to touch on Puig di Molins, Windmill Hill, where the view over the southern tip of the island was considerable, and where in an attractive little village amidst palms and fig trees, an old-fashioned water-wheel, with little tins and buckets to scoop the water from the well, was turned by a mule.

With the polished blue car cruising along leading the way, they continued on their tour of the island across to San Antonio Abad, the international holiday playground. Here the pavement cafés against the colourful harbour teemed with holiday life. Sun-bronzed figures were dressed in brilliant beach garb which ranged from the fashionable to the bizzare. There was an exuberant gaiety here unsubdued by the heat. The tree-lined promenade with gardens and fountains offered a change of scene for those in the mood to walk.

From San Antonio, the cars left the coast and headed for the countryside and the northern tip of the island. This was a beautiful run with citrus orchards and olive groves covering the hillsides. Among the orchards were the typical Ibizan arab-style houses and whitewashed farms. With the scent of juniper bushes filling the air, they climbed the road above a rocky bay, then descended in a series of bends to the shoreline of Portinax.

The beach of fine pale sand was lapped by a clear sea shot with a myriad tones of blues and greens. There was a scattering of villas amongst the trees. There were beach bars and hotels too. But Bruce carried on up the winding road until they came to an hotel whose terrace overhung the rocky coastline. Here he drew in and parked the car and waited for Francisco to join him.

Where cool white archways showed a panorama of sky and sea they found a table. For drinks, Mrs Kendall and Francisco agreed on *cafe con leche*, coffee with milk. Janet preferred *zumo de melocoton*, fresh peach juice with ice. Bruce ordered and chose Sangria for himself, a tall drink with ice.

Sitting across from him, noticing how his lean tanned features made a striking contrast against the blue of the sky, Janet felt a curious feeling of well-being.

Throughout the drive, with all the beauty of the island spread out before her, it had been impossible not to become alive a little, to feel the old glow inside herself returning. As each new scene turned up, begging to be enjoyed, she had found herself gradually waking up to the realisation that life after all was wonderful.

She knew that a little of the old light had returned to her eyes. Perhaps because of this she couldn't sit still opposite Bruce's blue gaze. As her mother chatted on to him gaily about the pretty setting of the hotel, and the people they had seen in San Antonio, she rose to join Francisco who was standing beside the archway.

In his friendly smiling way he pointed out the view of the bay of Portinax to her, and the colourful boats bobbing in front of the harbour houses. On the occasions when they had stopped along the way, during the drive, to climb the steps of some *mirador*, a look-out point, or to top the hill overlooking a panorama, Janet had found Francisco's conversation informative and they had often wandered off together to get a better glimpse of the view.

She stood with him and listened now as he laughingly told her about Cala Xarraca near by with its old smugglers cave right on the water's edge.

When the drinks were finished, and Dale had thoroughly investigated the flower pots around the terrace and the garden at the side, Janet and her mother went off to freshen up for the drive back. They had travelled in a full circle around the island so that it was now only thirty or forty kilometres home to San Gabrielle.

The sun's fiery glare was mellowing into the softer golden light of late afternoon when they met at the front of the hotel. Janet never knew how it came about that she and her mother changed places on the drive back. She wasn't sure whether it was Dale who took the initiative and jumped into Francisco's car by mistake, or whether Bruce had planned that the little orange car should lead the way on the return journey. At all events her mother settled in happily enough in the front vehicle, and Francisco gallantly attended to her needs before closing the door. Then with a wave for a signal they started off.

The polished blue car slid out after it and seated in cushioned comfort, aware of the slim brown hands on the wheel beside her, Janet had to admit she found the luxurious feel of the padded white upholstery distinctly soothing.

She had rinsed the dust of travel off her skin, combed up her hair into its usual soft waves and added a fresh touch of lipstick. Her white dress, smooth and unmarred in the iron grip of the heat, was but a gossamer weight against her body. As the breeze plucked at it gently with the car's motion, she felt strangely relaxed.

The little orange machine sped merrily ahead in front of them. They had negotiated the climb up from Portinax and were whispering along the deserted country highways towards San Gabrielle, when Janet was startled out of her restful reverie.

Whilst her gaze had been absently fixed ahead she felt the dark blue car suddenly change direction. The next second they were turning off on to a minor road, leaving Francisco's car to go speeding away into the distance on the main highway.

As he steered along the narrow route, Bruce gave no explanation for the move, except to mention casually, 'I have to see a client.'

Janet couldn't stir herself to react one way or the other. Her senses were dulled to everything but this peculiar contentment dragging at her limbs.

119

She wasn't tired of looking at the view. On the contrary, every tumbling wall, every crooked tree and faded blade of grass seemed to take on a new significance now as they invaded the country stillness together.

They had been travelling for perhaps ten or twenty minutes when the vista of the township they were presumably making for opened up suddenly in front of them. As they turned a bend in the road, a valley, yellow and mottled with farm fields and surrounded by humps of pine-clad hills, held in its palm a scattering of white houses which from a distance looked like a sprinkling of daisies in a grassy hollow.

The road descended and coursed like a river along the floor of the valley. Soon they were passing squat little dwellings half-screened by massive banks of prickly pear cactus, and walls festooned with tropical blossom.

Eventually they came to the narrow streets of the town. The car made its way slowly along the cool shadowed alleys until the houses hung together so close it seemed they must touch.

In a little open courtyard Bruce parked the car, and helping Janet out he commented, 'We have to walk from here.'

Their footsteps echoed over the tiles of the narrow passageways which he guided her along. The walls of the houses, white or pastel-tinted, rose high on either side of them. Above, overhanging bay windows were crowded with flower pots and trailing greenery, and on scroll bars fixed into the wall at intervals, the wrought-iron shapes of street lamps were etched against the narrow strip of blue sky.

On another street the houses were more imposing. They were spaced wider apart and the gateways had about them a certain old-world grandeur. It was at one of these gates that Bruce stopped to pull a bell which went pealing through the house. After a moment a woman in black came to the entrance. He handed her his card. She stared at it, then the merest flicker of recognition passing over her dour sun-

120

darkened features, she opened the iron gateway and bade them enter. Janet gathered that they had been asked to wait as the woman went upstairs.

The patio was pleasantly cool, the dark red tiles underfoot, soothing to the eye. There was about everything an air of dated prosperity. In the middle of the patio was a table with a solid rocking chair on either side of it. On the walls under the stairway were Spanish pictures, dark and glossy, and by the side of a door hung a pair of old pistols.

While they waited Bruce lit up a cigarette. Janet found the silence strangely disturbing. She knew a vague relief when at last a tall man appeared on the steps. He was old but agile with skin the colour of old ivory, and hair thick and white. He was dressed in black, and his eyes, equally black above a proud aquiline nose, shone with a fierce brilliance.

He reached the patio and Janet saw that he held in one hand a broad-brimmed hat. Though there was in his bearing a certain dignity, his manner suggested also a gentle humour.

She was introduced to Don Ignacio, who took her hand in his warmly and bowed in friendly fashion, after which Bruce went on in smiling but rapid Spanish.

Janet wondered about his business call. He had no briefcase with him. However, it seemed that conversation was enough to cover the points he had called about. She chose a seat near the stairs, leaving the two men to the rocking chairs on the patio, to hold their discussion.

On her own in the cool shadows, she expected to be there for some time, but after only a few minutes of amicable exchanges the men rose, their conversation apparently at an end.

Don Ignacio, with the true hospitality of the Spaniard, wanted to have wine brought and numerous other treats for his guests, all of which were charmingly refused, though Bruce Walbrook did make one casual request which

121

brought an eager response from the old man. With a smile he beckoned Janet, who had risen and was waiting to go, and leading the way he took them into a courtyard. From here they went along a narrow passage, then Janet found herself in an enchanting garden.

It was walled on three sides with walls as high as houses, and their old red brick, mellowed by time, was covered with roses. They clothed every inch in pastel-tinted scented luxuriance.

With his proud, gentle stoop, Don Ignacio led the way past palms rising high into the air in search of the sun, past dark orange trees, and other trees in flower, and among them roses and more roses.

Bruce's hand on her arm occasionally as they turned along a path, Janet was reminded of another time when she had walked in a garden with him. The villa garden. She felt an odd catch at her heart now at the memory, combined with an overwhelming ache at the beauty here.

The fourth wall was a Moorish loggia with horseshoe arches heavily festooned with hanging greenery. On its edge was a bench of Moorish tiles. One could imagine sitting here in the cool of the day and contemplating the tranquil scene of swallows darting and the sun slanting long shadows down the walls.

When they came back to the passage leading to the courtyard, after looking round the garden they took their leave of Don Ignacio. Janet smiled him her thanks. In return he bowed deeply over her hand, only too happy to have performed a kindness.

Bruce shook his hand, and as he did so the woman in black appeared. With the dignified but benign Spaniard waving them goodbye, they were shown into the street.

There were signs of life in the little town now that the heat of the day had abated a little. Shawled figures clung to the shadows along the passageways, and at one point Janet felt herself being drawn to a pause by Bruce's hand on her arm. A second later a string of little donkeys passed by. Their red caparisons were faded. She wondered what their bulging panniers held.

It was a charming scene, and as she watched them move on she began to see now why Bruce had turned off the main highway earlier on; why he had driven her here to this white town in the valley ... its narrow streets, tiled and cool, the houses cluttered with flower-pots and wrought-iron work, the proud black-clad figure of Don Ignacio, his beautiful garden ...

The man guiding her along beside him had gone out of his way to show her a true corner of Spain. She knew that now. But as they wandered on past silent doorways and stone-built alcoves, she reminded herself that he was simply trying to make amends for the death of their cat. As the Fords' attorney he no doubt shouldered the responsibility for damage done by villa guests and this would be his way of atoning for it.

Though Janet told herself this, she couldn't help feeling a tiny ache of pleasure inside her. When they came suddenly upon a small open space separating the narrow streets, she didn't know why she stopped. There was nothing here except bare walls and heavily barred windows. And yet one could almost hear the click of castanets, the rattle of tambourines on the sun-drenched stillness.

This odd ache growing inside her, she was filled with an urge to linger. Moving on her own, she drifted to where a centuries-old fountain, its cherubs chipped and disfigured with the passage of time, stood amidst the smell of hot dust. As she paused she let her gaze travel slowly around the sultry corners and shadowy stretches of the square. It was strange, but here more than anywhere she felt the primitive force of Spain.

Or perhaps it was just her own mood that created an atmosphere of age-old feuds and unsuppressed passion? She couldn't explain the potency of the stillness, except to say that her own feelings seemed to be tied up with it in some way.

She had walked away from Bruce, but he was beside her now. She wondered if this meant that he sensed a little of what she was feeling.

His nearness swelled that odd little ache inside her. She longed for the touch of his fingers on her arm. He had guided her round Don Ignacio's garden, led her through the streets of the town. Yet as the lowering sun brushed the misshapen cherubs briefly with gold, before bathing the square in deep shadow, he made no move to touch her now.

It was his gruff tones that broke the silence at last as he asked, 'Shall we go?'

'Yes.' As she drifted off with him, Janet realised it was the first word she had spoken to him all afternoon.

The car was parked in the next courtyard. She stepped into her seat as the door was opened for her. Within minutes they were leaving the narrow streets of the town and making for the highway back to San Gabrielle. With the white-walled tyres whispering along the traffic-free route, the breeze was left to make what it could of the silently cruising pair.

The warm air of dusk was heavy with the scent of villa blossom, when the car pulled up along the track. Janet had an urge to let herself out quickly, but Bruce was round to open the door for her before she could gather her things. She felt his lowered blue gaze on her as she stepped out against him, and was glad when the excited barking of Dale, and the appearance of her mother, gave her something else to think about.

She got to the terrace by feigning to fuss over the dog. The dark blue polished car slid on to park at the foot of the villa steps.

As Janet walked into the house, her mother was all fuss and laughter. Her hair awry, her finery discarded for an old cotton kimono, she raised her eyebrows and asked with a sly

124

gleam in her eyes, 'Well, what happened to you? Francisco brought me home ages ago.'

'Oh, we had to stop off to see a client,' Janet shrugged airily, and sailed away to her bedroom. She wanted to be alone with her thoughts; with this small glow in her heart.

Perhaps it was just her foolish imagination again, but looking back now to those heady moments beside the old fountain, it seemed to her that not only had she found them breathlessly disturbing. They had held something for Bruce too.

CHAPTER NINE

THERE was no postal service outside the boundaries of San Gabrielle. The mail was brought in every day on the afternoon bus, but the inhabitants of dwellings dotted over the countryside were obliged to call at the café in the village, or the *tienda de comestibles*, the grocer's shop, when they were expecting letters.

Mrs Kendall had to rely solely on someone passing on their way to the farm to receive mail from her family. As Janet had nothing special to do between six and seven in the evenings, she had got into the habit of strolling up to the village shop to collect whatever there was.

She arrived back one night as her mother was serving out the evening meal, and dropped the afternoon's delivery on the table. Mrs Kendall, always avid about the post, swooped on to the letters the moment she had put the pan in the sink. 'Oh, good, there's one from Ian. It's over a fortnight since I heard from him. And Jean,' she smiled fondly over her oldest daughter's handwriting, 'I expect she's telling me how little Jane got on at the ballet class.' Her eyes fell then on the stiff white envelope with the crest on the back of it. 'Why, what's this?' She held it up in the evening light. 'It's got a local stamp on it.'

'I wondered about that,' Janet said from where she was washing her hands at the sink. 'It's from someone on the island, obviously.'

'But I don't know anyone on the island, dear. Only the people around San Gabrielle.' Mrs Kendall turned the envelope over in her hand, both puzzled and fascinated.

'Why not open it, and then we'll find out what it is,' Janet smiled, knowing full well that no such thing would occur. She was familiar enough by now with the ritual that her mother adhered to.

The letters would stay unopened on the dining table to be eyed with pleasurable anticipation while the evening meal was being partaken of. They would then be moved to the rack beside the food cabinet while the washing up was in progress, and stay there until the kitchen had been tidied for the night. After which they would be transferred to the living room where they would be opened at leisure and perused over on and off until bedtime.

And so it was that it was well into the evening before they learned the contents of the crested envelope.

The lights were switched on in the living room. The red lamp shades here and there gave a cosy glow. Dale was sprawled out. The nights were far too stifling now for him to curl up in his basket. His favourite spot was on the cool tiles under the table.

They had to keep the door closed because of the numerous insects that came battering against the lamps. But with the shutters drawn it was possible to have the windows wide open on the inside. This made the indoors bearable.

Mrs Kendall was in her favourite armchair, her tortoiseshell glasses half way down her nose. Janet in old slacks and blouse was sprawled on the rug, her Spanish books spread out in the pool of light from the table. They had discussed the family letters from all angles, and she had long since lost interest in the crisp white envelope, when her mother, slitting it open at last, gave a little cry of pleasure.

She drew out a gilt printed card and Janet, her curiosity rekindled again, sat up to ask, 'What is it?'

'It's what everyone has been waiting for, my dear,' Mrs Kendall confided delightedly. 'The gala party of the season.'

She handed the card to Janet. The golden scroll on it asked for the pleasure of Mrs Kendall and her daughter's company over at the villa, on the afternoon of the twenty-ninth of July, a couple of days away.

'It looks as though it's going to be quite an occasion.' Janet handed the invitation back thoughtfully.

'Oh, I'm sure of it, dear,' her mother nodded, impressed. 'The Fords are very high up in the sea transport business. I hear there's going to be all kinds of shipping magnates there. The chairman of this beard and Sir Somebody-or other from that.' She smiled down with fresh delight at the card over the top of her glasses. 'How nice of Mr and Mrs Ford to send us an official invitation!'

'And through the post too,' Janet pointed out, musing over the envelope.

Twinkling along with her over the fact that they lived but half a dozen yards away, her mother said suddenly, 'Why don't you come over this time, Jan? I'm sure you'd find the experience well worth it.'

Janet didn't answer immediately. She had been toying with the idea ever since she had read the card, but not for the same reason as her mother.

It was over a week since she had seen Bruce. It was true she still caught glimpses of him going into the villa from his car occasionally, but ever since their afternoon drive there was a part of her that couldn't be content with this. She longed for an excuse to go over there. She was eager to create an opportunity similar to those she had known in Don Ignacio's garden, and beside the old fountain, where they could move close beside one another again.

The gala afternoon on Friday would give her the perfect excuse to go over to the villa. What more could she ask for than an official invitation?

She raised her head at last, having made up her mind, and replied gaily, 'All right! But I can't think what I'm going to do amongst a crowd of shipping magnates.'

'Oh, don't worry about that!' Mrs Kendall encouraged laughingly, pleased at her daughter's decision. 'The Fords like young people around them. There's bound to be a good

128

balance. There always is.'

Janet wasn't in the least worried. Bruce would be there. She doubted whether she would notice anyone else.

Her mother threw up her hands suddenly, her glasses jolting to the end of her nose. 'Heavens, I've just realised! I haven't got a thing to wear!'

Janet gave her a humorous look and shrugged, 'Oh, I expect you'll find something.'

Mrs Kendall, wearing a worried frown, was already rummaging mentally through the drawers and wardrobes in her bedroom. 'Well, I've got my dragon silk,' she pondered, brightening. 'It needs a couple of tucks in the side, but it's very modish ... quite dashing, in fact ... Yes!' She dropped everything and got up from her chair, inspired into action. 'I think I'll rout it out and see what I can do with it.'

Janet entered into preparation for the Villa party with something of the same eagerness during the next two days. She was anxious to look her best, and tossed all her dresses on to the bed in a fit of despondency. There seemed to be nothing at all to come up to the occasion. However, like her mother, she was obliged to have second thoughts and contented herself at last with a lilac dress, sleeveless and simple, but effective because of its tailored cut. Also its paleness contrasted well with the golden tan of her skin.

She washed her hair with an expensive shampoo, and spent hours browsing through her make-up box trying to decide on the right shade of lipstick.

Despite all her efforts, when she had showered and dressed carefully on the afternoon of the event, the end result was a simple summer look. But with her hair soft and shining, and the bloom of gold on her cheeks, she knew she was looking radiant, and she asked for nothing more.

Her mother had contrived to give a picture of startling elegance in her brilliantly patterned silk dress. The round high neck hugged her throat, vying with the vivid aquamarine pendant ear-rings that swung wildly when she talked.

As usual she was all for rushing over to the Villa on the stroke of the given time on the card, but Janet managed to delay the finishing touches to her own toilet until the track was lined with cars. They went right down, alongside the wall of the villa grounds today. She noticed, though, with a little stab of joy in her heart, that the dark blue polished car was parked in its usual place at the foot of the steps.

The gathering sounded to be quite a size as she and her mother crossed the tiled square at the top of the steps. She had been prepared for something a little extra special today, but nothing like that which met her eyes when they turned the corner of the villa.

The whole grounds were a riot of colour, as people dressed in all manner of summer fashion surged around specially arranged tubs of exotic flowers and rose trees. Sprigs of hanging blossom had been intertwined around the porticoed entrance of the villa, and other delicate splashes festooned hoops over the damask-clothed tables.

Amongst the pyramids of food and glinting silverware, white-coated stewards weaved with precariously-balanced trays, making excursions back and forth to the far corners of the garden and to the flower-decked tables beside the pool. A gold silk marquee had been erected on the side lawn along with endless other things that were too much to take in at a glance.

Mrs Kendall wasted no time in starting out to explore their surroundings, and Janet, a little shy now that she was over here, tagged thankfully alongside her. They ran into Mr Ford as they were making for the marquee. In his hearty friendly way he dropped an arm round each one of them and introduced them separately to every one of his friends grouped in the shade of a tree. Though the names were high-sounding, the men, red-faced and summer-clad, looked far less forbidding than they probably would have done if one had faced them, say, across a business conference table.

Drinks in hand, they were content enough now to exchange jaunty pleasantries and laugh gustily at each other's weak jokes. After a few minutes in their company, Janet and her mother left them and continued on their way.

They discovered on arrival that the gold silk marquee housed a small dance floor, shaded from the sun. The music drifting out was from a five-piece band, the musicians in black trousers and red shirts played happily for the half dozen or more couples who drifted chatteringly around the floor. There was a steward at the door to offer all newcomers a sparkling drink. The only thing to do for the moment seemed to be to stand inside sipping and watching the fun.

After this they strolled past another tent which was showing a travelogue made by one of the shipping magnates, and further on, around a circular platform a knot of people were watching a display of flamenco dancing.

They stayed on the lawn quite a while, then Mrs Kendall, itching for a chat, drifted off towards the buffet tables. Janet, her gaze raking the groups, moved down towards the pool. Though there was an impromptu game of water polo in progress, she had no eyes for it.

Ever since she had arrived she had been keyed up, her senses poised for the moment when she would spot Bruce. She was still keyed up. He wasn't out here. She knew he was in the villa and wondered why he chose to work this afternoon of all days. She wished he would hurry up and come out and join the party.

She noticed too, a little wistfully, that Francisco wasn't here either. But she needn't have worried about being on her own, for it was a lively crowd around the pool. Without any attempts on her part she was soon part of a laughing group who were pushing, or being pushed dangerously near to the edge of the water.

Two strapping Scandinavians came to Janet's rescue. They were mature young men, probably on their way up in the shipping business, but not too serious to enjoy the fun in progress. They took it upon themselves to steer Janet away from the skirmish unscathed. After a drink with them and one or two others, she drifted with the group up to the far lawn for a game of croquet.

The hoops were arranged on the strip of grass adjoining the villa terrace. As it turned out, the men were much more superior at the game than the girls, though there was little serious play as no one was in the mood to obey the rules. Janet, as bad as everyone else, was laughingly trying for a hoop when her pivoting glance caught a glimpse of a familiar lean figure standing beside one of the buffet tables.

Her heart spun. The ache that had kept it tense all afternoon suffused her insides and sped to her eyes in the form of a joyful glow.

Her first reaction was to drop everything. With Sven and Emil beside her, however, urging her on with the hilarities of the games, there was little opening for her to leave. She had to wait until the fun petered out and everybody's mind turned towards food.

Emil, his great arm across her shoulders, guided her amidst the group to a table only a stone's throw from where Bruce stood. As he chatted to a Spanish couple, she noticed he was wearing one of those impeccable tropical-style suits which he used for business. She had been right about him choosing to work today. Still, what did it matter? He was here now.

She couldn't eat, of course. Though her plate was piled with all manner of succulent bits from the array of food, all she wanted was a chance to drift off on her own with Bruce. He had seen her, she knew. She had felt his eyes on her when she had been on the lawn, which must have been from the moment he had stepped out of the villa. And she hadn't missed his hard gaze just now, a look somehow that turned her heart over.

She longed for the time when he would be able to terminate his conversation with the couple, and gradually she

132

put herself on the edge of the party she was with, timing it so that they would both be free at the same second.

At last, flicking her glance in that direction, she saw the Spanish pair making to move off. Pretending to be sharing in the volatile conversation which was going on beside her, she held the moment, every nerve in her body straining for that touch on her arm. She waited at such a pitch she convinced herself that she had heard those deep casual tones behind her. But when she turned, just as casually, she found it was an elderly lady who had been asking her if she would reach her some smoked salmon.

Still smiling, Janet obliged, letting her glance wander lightly round the crowd as she did so. She saw with a sudden empty feeling that the spot where Bruce had been standing was deserted.

After another lightning flick around, her gaze searched him out. He was over on the far side of the terrace now, talking amidst a lively group.

Her heart, which had been flying so high, suddenly lost the use of its wings. She found it difficult to keep the smile on her face. Fortunately, one of the men near the table, noticing that she was on her own, joined her with his drink. She was glad to put on a show of laughing at the jokes he tossed at the rest of the crowd. At least she had the fun around her to cling to while she struggled with the rawness which was a pain inside her.

This ought to be a lesson to her, she told herself. In future she would have to remember to stick strictly to business. As a mere woman she had been content to let her heart rule her head, pushing all thoughts of the fight for the track out of her mind. What a fool she had been to think that Bruce could forget it for one minute! That was why he had chosen to work today to let her see that as a hard-hitting lawer he was interested in only one thing, winning his case for his clients. Oh, she knew that he watched her from a distance. But he was letting her see also that that was as far as he was prepared to let it go.

She joined in the laughter going on about her. Thank heavens she had given no sign that she had even noticed him. Mercifully she had kept her feelings to herself, so that now she could carry on an animated conversation with the man beside her as though it was the most important thing in the world to her.

She had no idea how she got through the rest of the afternoon. Perhaps she smiled a little too brightly at times. Perhaps she talked a little too much. Her only concern was in keeping up the gaiety until the party came to an end.

She felt physically weary by the time the first of the cars started to leave. She was bound to stay on with the Scandinavian group she had made friends with, but at last when they drifted across the square she was able to make use of their company to the gate.

She didn't give a backward glance to where Bruce stood with another departing group, though she knew his gaze followed her as she left.

Carefree as ever on the surface, she waved the cars off, then swung lightly over to the house. Even there she wouldn't let herself give in to her aching disappointment. She flung the door wide, and gave Dale a run round the garden after he had been cooped up all afternoon.

She was in the kitchen filling the kettle when her mother came in, worn out but flushed and full of chat about the party. She unscrewed her tremendous ear-rings as she gave a detailed account of all the people she had spoken to. She had spent a few pleasant minutes with Mrs Ford, and it turned out that Lady Whatever-her-name-was was really a very sweet person ... stopping for breath her mother took off her shoes and letting her stockinged feet spread luxuriously on the cool tiles, she came up to ask,

'Did *you* have a good time, dear?'

'Fabulous!' Janet lied, lunging for cups and saucers with a brilliant smile.

Her mother gave her a searching look and added, as she unfastened the belt of her dress, 'I didn't see much of Bruce. Did you?'

Janet hunted noisily for tea spoons in the drawer. 'He was around somewhere, I believe.' She tried to sound nonchalant as she turned to the boiling kettle.

Just as she had been, her mother was suffering from the delusion that Bruce had other things on his mind beside the track.

CHAPTER TEN

THE tiny beach at the Playa del Mitx was far too crowded now with holidaymakers to think of going there. And yet after the villa party Janet felt a need to get away from the house.

Most days she started out after lunch in cotton slacks and thin blouse, sun-hat shading her eyes, and refreshments packed in a picnic bag. On one of her walks she had discovered a path directly opposite the farm track on the other side of the main road, which meandered up the pine-clad hill overlooking the house, on the right. It was really a small mountain, but with the pines growing very thickly for shade it was possible to reach the top, taking it in stages. And as the path was well trodden it was obviously a popular walk.

As it was much higher than the village hill the views of the surrounding plain were even more fantastic. At the very top was a stone monument erected by the villagers, who could say how many scores of year ago?

On the other side of the monument the ground fell sharply away, slicing into a canyon formed by an adjoining hill. If one had a mind to go on, a narrow path, starting between two high rocks, coursed leisurely down to the floor of the canyon and continued on through almond groves and strips of cultivated land. There were caves in the rocks at this side if one lifted one's glance. Some had been made into grottoes and white stone figures looked out over the valley from the openings.

Janet could always find plenty to keep her occupied around these parts, and the unbroken peace, with nothing to disturb the silence but the fleeting song of a bird, or the buzz of an insect, was a soothing influence on her flat spirits.

It was one afternoon when she was crossing the main road on one of these excursions that she ran into Tollo, or rather, he almost ran into her. She had always known that his driving left a lot to be desired ever since he had driven her round to the school that day. Hw was young, and still a little drunk with the power of owning his own car, even though it was little more than a wreck. She had seen him once or twice tearing about the village, but this was the first time she had met him along the main road.

With his big gappy smile, and the flamboyant way he had of swinging the wheel, he screeched to a stop only inches from her trousered legs. Slamming out, he greeted her in that sedate English of his which was totally out of keeping with his rough country look.

'Hello there!'

'Hello, Tollo,' Janet replied laughingly. It was always impossible not to become infected with this live-wire air he radiated.

Itching to be of service, he swaggered beside his car with a proprietorial manner and offered, 'Can I give you a lift into town?'

'No, thanks,' Janet smiled. 'I'm just off for a walk.' To make conversation she asked, 'Are you going to work?'

'Yes,' Tollo nodded, 'just for three hours, and then I shall be finished for the day.'

Janet hesitated for a moment. Come to think of it, it *would* make a change to go into town. Apart from the weekly shopping visits with her mother she never went there, and three hours was no longer than the time she spent roaming the countryside on her lone walks.

'Does that mean you'll be driving back as soon as you've finished?' she asked thoughtfully.

'But of course!' Tollo nodded, reading her mind. 'I can take you and bring you back if you like.'

Janet did some quick thinking. She wasn't dressed for town of course. Her old cotton slacks and cheap celanese blouse had been donned strictly to do battle on a rough climb. But they were colourful enough. And who worried on a holiday island?

She had her picnic bag, plus her purse, which she always carried with her in case of emergencies, so there was really no reason why she shouldn't accept Tollo's offer of a ride. Besides, she had an urge to try and beat this flatness inside her, and with sudden recklessness she tossed her head, and said gaily, 'All right, Tollo. You can take me to town.'

With his clumsy flair, the young Spaniard opened the door for her. Wincing at the sight of it, Janet took the lop-sided seat that showed most of its flock insides, and settled precariously with her bag on her knee.

She had always considered the ride on the local bus a hair-raising journey, but compared to Tollo's driving it was a mere stroll. They tore round bends and leapt over pot-holes as though they were competing in some mad race. She noticed as he swung the wheel indolently as though it had no more power in it than a toy pedal car, that they spread themselves all over the road when they took a curve. She shuddered to think what would happen if something should be coming the other way. Fortunately there was never that much traffic about. Only the wealthy brought their cars to the island, so the road for the most part was deserted. Also she consoled herself with the fact that Tollo must have been doing this journey for some time now.

The town was in the throes of siesta time when they arrived. The shops were shut, and the cafés, steeped in a drowsy air, were patronised mainly by the locals. The holi-daymakers were probably panting in the heat in their hotels or cooling themselves off on the beaches.

Tollo drove through the narrow streets with care now, for there were white-shirted traffic policemen about. His place of employment, the Hotel Morocco, was a tall, glossy painted section, sandwiched between a line of similar gay exteriors which ran the length of a small *calle* just off the tree-shaded square. He parked a little way along because the area was full of other vehicles, and with his usual panache invited Janet into the hotel for a drink.

There were a handful of tables on the small terrace shaded by fringed umbrellas, and because she had nothing special to do Janet drifted along with him.

It was pleasant enough sitting watching the sleepy life in the square a few yards away. When she had finished her drink she went in to see Tollo at work.

In his place at the reception desk he was busy sorting out traveller's cheques and currency notes. Though he had changed from his casual country garb, the neat black suit he wore now did nothing to tone down his cheeky grin, which was as blatant as ever.

Janet left her picnic bag with him, taking with her just her purse and her handkerchief, and arranged to meet him at the corner of the *calle* when he had finished work. She had no idea how she was going to spend the time. She supposed she might as well do a little sight-seeing. She drifted off without much enthusiasm towards the quay.

There she stared at the view of the houses rising steeply across the slope of the hill, and at the sandstone cathedral dominating the skyline. From the quay she wandered to the fishing quarter where there were whitewashed cottages. She saw the walls of the old town, drifted past buildings decorated with frescoes and coloured tiles, and scuffed along the wide Paseo lined with shady trees, plants and flowers. It was thirsty work walking, however, and she was glad to give it up after a while for a seat at a café overlooking the quay. She lazed here until it was time to go back and meet Tollo.

With the opening of the shops and the slackening of the heat, the town had become alive with people. When Janet arrived at the tree-shaded square the scene had changed completely. In contrast to the deserted look of mid-afternoon, everything was now noise, gaiety and bustle.

Business men in shirt-sleeves were doing deals at café tables. Lobster-pink holidaymakers sat over tall drinks, engaged in laughing conversation. Children darted under the trees. There were the cries of the lottery ticket sellers outside the shops, the rumble of traffic, the raised voices of the pavement waiters clashing with the chatter of black-shawled old ladies, bartering for the evening's food. In fact, all the pandemonium of a Spanish square after siesta time.

Janet pushed her way round to the street of the Hotel Morocco, losing quite a few minutes in the crush, so that she arrived a little late. She saw Tollo's car immediately. He had driven it up to the corner facing on to the square in readiness for leaving, and seeing that she wasn't about had probably strolled off for a moment. She looked down the street towards the hotel, but the entrance was crowded with holidaymakers. She decided to wait by the car.

At last she saw Tollo coming along the busy street. He was in the company of several youths of his own age, all perhaps having finished work at the same time. Their laughter was bawdy as they strolled swaggeringly up to the square. On arriving they made loud derogatory remarks about Tollo's old car, all of which he took in good part, smiling with them as they hung around it.

It was while Janet was waiting in their noisy midst for Tollo to bid them goodbye that her heart suddenly spiralled up into her throat.

Her abstracted gaze, roaming the crowds, had come upon a lean tanned figure, briefcase in hand, standing only a couple of streets away, in the square. In his faultlessly tailored summer suit, Bruce was talking to a briefcase-carrying associate. She remembered that the law offices were around here somewhere and that he parked his car along one of these streets. Aware almost at once that his hard blue gaze was fixed on her, she turned quickly away.

What she must look like in old slacks and blouse,

tumbling into Tollo's broken-down old car—for he was now holding the door for her—amidst a bunch of rowdy uncouth youths, she didn't dare imagine. But tossing her head and telling herself that what she did with her time was entirely her own affair, she laughed along with the Spanish boys, and made herself a part of the general air of merriment.

When at last Tollo dragged himself away from his friends, closed her door, and lumbered round into his own seat, Janet didn't give a sideways look at a certain chiselled profile. She made sure that she was chattering gaily to Tollo when the old car trundled off.

As usual her young companion drove erratically through the streets of the town. More than once she thought they would catch it from the traffic authorities for cutting corners and ignoring signs, but with all the other drivers doing much the same and yelling '*Burro!*' at one another from their car windows, as one after the other touched bumpers in heavy traffic, Tollo wasn't on his own.

Janet didn't know whether to be relieved or sorry when they headed out into the country on the San Gabrielle highway. It was debatable whether his crazy driving in the town was preferable to the unobstructed speed of the open road.

Lazily flicking the wheel, Tollo was happily giving her a run-down on his afternoon's activities. Not wishing to take his mind off the wheel Janet listened in smiling silence.

They were well out into the country, hurtling along. She didn't know what prompted her to look in the rust-mottled mirror just above the windscreen. When she did, she saw a familiar dark polished car following not far behind them.

Her brown eyes smouldered with reckless satisfaction. So Bruce hadn't wasted much time in driving off after them! She had a vague suspicion he had tailed them on their mad jaunt through town and her lips pulled into an amused curl. That must have cost him something in avoiding the dents in his own sleek conveyance!

They tore round the bends. Though they were moving at

141

a wild pace, the dark blue car remained steadily in view in the overhead mirror. There was no question of such a powerful model needing to put on speed to keep up with them. It was rather like a sleek panther following effortlessly in the tracks of a bucking, frantic rabbit.

Tollo had no idea of the existence of the other car, of course. It was doubtful whether he had looked in his rear mirror more than half a dozen times during his driving life. Janet left him to his ignorance and pretended not to notice herself. Why should *she* care if they were being followed?

She had arranged to be dropped off at the top of the farm road where Tollo had picked her up earlier in the afternoon. They came up to it now and the car slowed down to a stop just past it. Janet didn't get out straight away. She stayed purposely chatting to Tollo until the dark blue car slid up. It turned in slowly and crunched along on its way to the villa.

She pretended to be totally oblivious of its existence, giving all her attention blithely to what Tollo had to say. She learned that he would be working these hours for the next few weeks. Up very early in the morning, back home for a long siesta, and then returning to work for three hours in the afternoon.

'Tomorrow I have a day off.' He rounded off the conversation. 'But the day after I can pick you up at the same time if you like?'

Janet thought about it. She hadn't found the afternoon in town particularly exciting. Still, it was somewhere different to go, she supposed. And no doubt she would get used to Tollo's atrocious driving in time.

'All right!' she thanked him, laughing. 'I'll wait for you here at the usual time.'

She left him then and watched him tear off impudently on his way, quite happy to be acting as chauffeur for *los ingles*.

As she went down the farm road she decided it might be

best if she didn't mention the afternoon's events or her plans to her mother. She would only worry if she knew her daughter was careering off to town most afternoons in a decrepit old car.

Picnic bag in hand, passing the villa, Janet saw the dark blue conveyance parked inside the gates. Musing over the hectic ride from town, she noticed with an acid gleam the car's thick coating of dust.

She went up the track and entered the house with the air of having spent the afternoon climbing the pine-clad hills.

On the day she was due to meet Tollo again it was necessary to keep up this illusion, so she donned old slacks and blouse and packed her picnic bag as before. In any case she felt too low-spirited to want to dress up. Slopping around in old clothes suited her mood these days.

She was up at the top of the farm track in good time. To be sure of not missing the old car she stood on the roadside in the glare of the sun. However, after ten minutes of this she had to retire into the shade of the big carob tree. She could still see the route from the village beneath the leaves. She waited. Not so much as a farm cart passed in the following ten minutes.

After half an hour she looked at her watch. Funny that she hadn't seen any car pass. Tollo was due to start work within the next few minutes, so he must have gone. And yet she had left the house with plenty of time to spare. She couldn't imagine how she had missed him.

She waited another quarter of an hour just in case he had been held up somewhere. Then swinging up her bag, she crossed the road and scuffed off along the pine-clad path. It really made little difference to her. She was just as content to idle around the countryside, and she could always catch Tollo tomorrow.

To be absolutely sure she didn't miss him the following afternoon she got up to the road twenty minutes before he

143

was due to pass. She waited in the shade of the carob tree. The minutes ticked by. Exactly the same as yesterday, the road remained deserted. Not a thing moved to disturb the shimmering silence of the afternoon.

Janet frowned to herself. She couldn't fathom what had become of Tollo. Even if he had forgotten he was taking her to town she would have seen him pass. She knew there was another smaller road leading out of the village which linked up with the main road further on. But why would he take that route? Drifting off on her usual stroll, she decided to tackle him about it, when she saw him again.

The opportunity presented itself that same evening.

During the day the islanders hid from the sun as though they feared it would strike them down on the spot. It was at night-time that the villages came alive. And San Gabrielle was no exception. As soon as the cool shadows dropped over the hillside it awoke to become the scene of noise and activity.

Children whooped up and down the *calles* and tethered dogs barked uproariously because they couldn't join in the fun. Mothers supervised their toddlers from their doorways exchanging domestic chat with neighbours in raucous voices. The men tinkered with carts and farm machinery in tumble-down flower-strewn courtyards or loafed about the café tables in the Plaza. The young men of the village congregated around their possessions of old scooters and cars, wherever it was convenient.

Janet was familiar with the scene, as she came into San Gabrielle most evenings to pick up the mail. It was when she was leaving the *comestibles* with the afternoon's delivery of letters that she saw that Tollo had joined the group of youths on the corner of the square.

He didn't seem in the least perturbed to see her. In fact he strolled to meet her in his brash clumsy way, his broken-toothed smile as wide as ever.

Janet returned his friendly greeting, then tilting an eye-

144

brow at him she asked wryly, 'What happened to my transport this afternoon? And yesterday? I thought you were going to give me a lift into town?'

'Oh . . .' Tollo shrugged his shoulders with a sheepish grin, 'it wasn't possible. I am sorry.'

'Well, that's all right,' Janet smiled. She turned her puzzled glance over his vehicle parked at the side of them and asked, 'But your car's not broken down, is it?'

Tollo looked more sheepish than ever as he shook his head. He shuffled about. His grin slanted and he lowered his eyes over an impudent light. He admitted at last, 'It was the *señor* at the villa. He say . . .' Tollo brought his finger across his throat and made an appropriate slicing sound.

Janet hadn't the faintest notion what he was talking about. Her gaze becoming more puzzled, she looked to him and asked, 'But I don't understand. Which *señor* at the villa?'

'The *abogado*. The lawyer who drives the fast car into town,' came the lazy reply.

Bruce! With a stirring of something like anger inside her, Janet was beginning to understand. 'Well, what has he been saying to you?' she demanded hotly.

Tollo tilted his head in a bemused way as he replied, 'To use his English words, I think he said he would break my neck if I drove you in my car again.'

Janet's anger exploded into two spots of colour in her cheeks. 'Well, what a nerve!' She fumed at what she'd heard. And to her young companion she said feelingly, 'Look, Tollo. This English lawyer, Bruce Walbrook—he has got nothing whatsoever to do with me. If I want you to take me to town it's no concern of his.' And with a sudden rush of defiance she added, 'I'd like you to take me tomorrow, if you would.'

'All right,' Tollo grinned, not in the least put out that she was asking him to stick his neck into a noose. 'But what shall I say if the *señor* comes looking for me in the village

145

again?'

'You can tell him from me that it's none of his business.' Janet said crossly. She softened her mood to bid Tollo goodbye, and as he waved her off down the hill she called out to him over her shoulder, smiling, 'See you tomorrow afternoon, about the same time.'

Making her way back home, she felt a stab of apprehension when she thought over what she had done. Quickly she shrugged it off. She didn't see why she should calmly suffer Bruce's interference in her life. And anyway, Tollo, with his carefree attitude and impudent smile, wasn't likely to be too unnerved by anything that Bruce said.

The following afternoon she dressed as usual in old clothes as though she were going roaming the countryside and swinging up her picnic bag she set off up to the main road. She hadn't been waiting long under the carob tree when Tollo came swerving along from the village.

He stopped with his usual eagerness to help her, greeting her as though he hadn't a care in the world. She dropped into the seat beside him of the same accord and together they went careering off along the road on their wild dash into town.

When they arrived, Janet was of the opinion that she must be growing accustomed to Tollo's abominable driving. Either that or she was just too dazed by the experience to react one way or the other.

Having no particular desire to go sightseeing, she spent half the afternoon sitting with a magazine on the terrace of the hotel Morocco. The other half she spent wandering around the shops as they opened.

She felt hot and dusty when she got back to the square. Waiting for Tollo on the corner amidst the accelerating noise and crush of holidaymakers didn't help. When he arrived she asked him if he would mind if she stayed to have a drink first as she was absolutely dying of thirst. As if a Spaniard would grumble at the chance to while away the time at a pavement café!

Naturally Tollo had no objections and happily led the way to the tables on the corner beside the car. He was too gauche to know how to proceed in her company. Janet paid for his drink as well as her own.

Though she had quenched her thirst from time to time during the heat of the afternoon with the orange crush in her picnic bag, nothing tasted so wonderful now as this tall glass of ice-cool liquid with the straw bobbing at her touch. They drank leisurely, watching the lively activity in the square. To add to it, just as they were finishing, Tollo's youthful pals came drifting along the *calle* towards them. Without a care for originality they made the same derisive comments, all strolling around his broken old car with mocking grins.

Janet gathered that this was a regular performance every night and she took it with the same humour as Tollo. She really wasn't too concerned with the antics of the young Spanish boys. Most of her attention was taken up, and had been since arriving, with the business of surreptitiously searching the crowds with her gaze, for signs of a familiar figure.

Half of her was in fear of spotting Bruce. The other half of her blatantly wanted to be seen, purely as a gesture of defiance. She was beginning to think that she was going to be deprived of that pleasure. On the corner Tollo had opened the rickety door of his car for her, and she was dropping into what was just an excuse for a seat amidst the good-natured taunts and jostlings of his mates. Just as she was laughing at the commotion her glance swung on to that lean tanned face only a street away.

Who Bruce was with she had no idea. She could just make out his dark head and smooth-clad shoulders as he stood surrounded by the passers-by. One thing she *was* sure of. His gaze was riveted on her. Even from this distance she could see the taut anger on his face as he watched her in the

147

midst of the rough play.

Dusty and dishevelled, she tossed her head at him, prolonging her laughter and ignoring the haphazard thumping of her heart. Too bad if he didn't like the idea of her scruffing around town in Tollo's old car. It happened to suit *her*!

For all her bravado she was glad when at last her young friend started up and they jerked off to make their way through the busy streets of the town.

As she had half expected, once they were out on the San Gabrielle road the dark blue car came nosing in behind them. She was sure Tollo hadn't seen it. His youthful mind on other things, he hung over the wheel, occasionally bursting into a snatch of Spanish pop song as he tore along the stretch of road.

The dark car didn't overtake them. Though it could easily have eaten up their speed, it stayed behind, following in their swerving bouncing path like some marauding animal.

By the time they reached the farm road Janet was feeling rather limp from the strain. She asked Tollo to drive past a little way and breathed a deep sigh of relief when the polished car swung slowly in a second or two later and crunched off down the farm road.

She watched it out of the back of her head as it were, but once it had disappeared from view she felt considerably irritated with herself and her nervous state. To offset her shakiness she recklessly arranged to meet Tollo again the next day.

She spent a restless evening wondering how he was faring in the village. But if Bruce had been up there again to rap him for his disobedience, he gave no sign of it the following afternoon. Apart from a trace of paleness beneath his dark complexion, he was his usual clumsy, grinning self. Janet guessed that he had given Bruce her message as she had told him to. She half suspected that his defiance was as strong as her own, in a harmless cheeky kind of way.

148

Most afternoons, after that, found them slewing along the country roads to town, and back again at tea time. Though Janet was well aware that she was watched on the occasions when she met Tollo in the square, she gave no sign of this. The man with a muscle flexing in the jaw of his tanned features, as he followed her movements with his narrowed blue gaze, was just part of the crowd as far as she was concerned. Or so she blithely made it appear.

She became accustomed to seeing Bruce's car trailing them when they careered madly back along the road home. Sometimes when the drive was particularly hectic she thought the dark shape moved in a little as though to come alongside them.

On the other hand this could have been purely her imagination. She did tend to be living on her nerves these days. Tollo's wildness behind the wheel took some coping with, and the jaunts to town had done nothing to help her weighted spirits. If anything they were having the opposite effect. It was all very well pretending to be having a gay time just to defy Bruce, but seeing him every day only made matters worse. She didn't know how much longer she could keep up this pseudo-adventure without breaking in two.

Strangely enough, the glimpses she caught now and again of Bruce's taut features told her that she wasn't alone in feeling the strain.

Then something happened one afternoon that brought the whole thing to a head. Tollo's driving, the source of much of the friction between them, was responsible for what occurred just a couple of miles out of San Gabrielle.

Without an inkling that disaster was round the corner Janet was sitting listening to the description of a film Tollo had seen the night before. The islanders lacked the sophistication of city filmgoers. After a night at the cinema they could talk of nothing else the next day. They re-lived every scene of the film with all the actions for the benefit of their friends, insisting on telling the story from beginning to end.

Janet was getting the full treatment now as Tollo rode a galloping horse in an exciting race. His head down, his hands on the wheel holding the imaginary reins, first he was on the winning horse, then he was on the one coming up behind. When he couldn't find the right words in English he lapsed into excited Spanish.

Janet gave most of her attention to her young companion's story, because she found it took her attention off his atrocious driving.

The loaded cart taking up most of the narrow road round the bend ahead was as much of a surprise to her as it was to him.

If they had been going at a reasonable pace it would have been simply a matter of slowing down to follow the cart round the bend before overtaking it. As it was there was no time for that.

Her gaze caught a flash of the piles of pine brushwood stacked high on the rumbling cart, then Tollo was jumping on the brakes and they were screeching and squealing to miss it by inches and heading for a bank at the side of the road. They shuddered up it—how they avoided overturning Janet never knew—and shuddered down it again, and after much skidding and squealing around the rest of the bend they found themselves on the straight road ahead once more.

With typical Spanish disregard for danger Tollo grinned, not a little pleased at having shown the old cart who was boss. It was probably his complete lack of nerves that had got them through without mishap, but Janet couldn't share his nonchalant attitude. She was too conscious of the fact that if luck hadn't been on their side they could have been involved in a very nasty accident.

She shuddered when she recalled the sound of the screaming brakes. They had probably been heard all over the countryside. She thought of the dark polished car which she

150

remembered had been in its usual position just a little way behind them. Bruce would be held up back there. He wouldn't take the risk that Tollo had taken, in bypassing a loaded cart on a bend.

She was glad of the breathing space to get to the house before he appeared. As soon as they stopped at the top of the farm road she tumbled out of the old car, amazed at the weakness in her legs. She watched Tollo swing off with whistling unconcern towards the village, then blundered off along the farm track with as much speed as her shaky legs would allow.

She wasn't fast enough, however, for just as she reached the villa gates she heard the ominous sound of a car swerving in on a squeal of brakes on to the farm road. She struggled on, ignoring the speeding vehicle which was approaching behind her.

She got to the railway track and stumbled along the length of its rocky surface, in time to hear the whoosh of the car swerving in on two wheels after her. She was on the terrace. The car braked hard in a shudder of dust at the side of her. She heard the ear-shattering slam of a door. She reached the patio. The sharp sound of striding footsteps came after her. Her heart thumping in her throat, Janet hurried indoors. She heard her mother working in the kitchen and fled to her, but as the sound of those footsteps came closer across the patio she stayed no longer than it took her to gasp, 'I'll go and see if there are any eggs,' and fled out of the back door leaving her mother open-mouthed over the pastry she was mixing.

How Janet got down the meadow she was never really sure. As she walked, or half-ran along the path, her nervousness giving her wings, she tried to ignore the striding footsteps that had followed her out of the house.

Down at the hen enclosure, striving to put on a natural air, she snatched up a basin and with trembling fingers searched out three or four eggs. Because she couldn't trust

151

herself to hold them once she had gathered them, she stuck them on top of a square post beside the chicken run, then paced around. She was pretending to be vitally interested in the distant scenery when the striding footsteps came up behind her.

Bruce didn't bother with any preliminaries. His voice shaking in an odd way, he rapped, 'If you've got any more plans for riding in that broken-down excuse for a car, you can forget them!'

'Oh?' Quiveringly Janet swung on him. 'Since when have I been having my mind made up for me?'

'Since right now,' he fired back.

Janet's pulses hammered in her throat. Though she knew her own face was white with strain, it came as a cold shock to see Bruce's face, pale and working too.

To cover up her dilemma, she made an attempt at flippancy, saying airily, 'That's funny! I expect to be going to town as usual tomorrow. In fact I'm quite looking forward to the ride.'

Bruce took a step forward. She thought he was either going to hit her or shake her. His voice menacingly low, he got out, 'You realise you could have ended up in a heap back there just now, don't you?'

Janet saw the flames of something like anger in his eyes. She met them with her own unsteady gaze and gave a careless shrug to toss back at him, 'But we didn't. And anyway, why should that be any concern of yours?'

'Because, you young fool——' As though something exploded inside him he grabbed her. His fingers sinking into her flesh made her wince with pain, but before she could cry out, he had pulled her roughly against him and dropped his mouth on hers.

Janet, for a moment, saw stars at the savage move. Then gradually when she realised what was happening, the stars began to mellow blissfully into soft pink glows all around her, and her body, mellowing too, relaxed slowly against the hard lean frame. For long enough she experienced a sweetness that she had never known before, as the taut mouth fastened itself demandingly on hers. She wanted the world to stop there, just as it was.

Then, becoming slowly aware that her arms had somehow found their way up and were curved around the linen-suited shoulders, she drew away with a rush of colour. It took her a few moments to find her legs, and brushing the wisps of hair from her face for the sake of something to do, she stammered with stars of a different kind in her eyes now, 'I think . . . I'd better be getting back to the house.'

Bruce watched her move away. Perhaps it was something he had found out for himself that made him slope a smile. Handing her the bowl from the top of the fence post, he said whimsically, 'Don't forget your eggs.'

Janet took them and floated up the path back to the house, while lazy footsteps crunched away across the track.

Mrs Kendall was standing at the back door, flour caked on her arms, her hair up on end, just as she had left the kitchen to see what the sudden flow of traffic through the house was all about. The puzzled look which had been stamped on her features had slowly been giving way to one of surprise, mingled with a sneaking delight. Now as she watched Janet move into the house, an enigmatic smile on her face, she expressed her reaction at what she had just seen at the bottom of the meadow in one volubly explosive word,

'Well!'

Janet, blushing under her teasing gaze, laughed shyly with shining eyes, 'Oh, Mother!' and made a quick escape to her bedroom.

She didn't walk. She was transported on a rainbow-coloured cloud accompanied by the music playing in her heart.

He had kissed her. Bruce had actually kissed her!

CHAPTER ELEVEN

AUGUST was the month for fiestas in Ibiza. Because of the heat the afternoon parties at the villa had come to an end. The fashion now was to travel in the cool of the evening to whichever village was celebrating its saint's day, and have one's party there—not very difficult when the villagers in question spared themselves nothing to make theirs the gayest *pueblo* of them all.

The *calles* were sure to be decorated from end to end with gay flags and banners. There was music and dancing, wine to drink, and all the local colour one could want at one's fingertips. The Fords usually went with a small crowd of friends. Mrs Kendall had been a couple of times in with their group.

The morning following the meadow incident Janet returned from a shopping expedition to the village to find her mother waiting for her impatiently on the terrace.

'Bruce was over while you were away,' she said, smiling conspiratorially, 'but he had to leave for town. The Fords are going over to Santa Margarita tonight. He brought us an invitation to join their party.'

Janet's heart skipped a beat. Bruce had been across to the house and she had missed him. Still, she would probably have been too shy to look him in the eye anyway. She heard her mother's news with mixed feelings. Was Bruce going to the fiesta? Well, of course he must be, she told herself, otherwise he wouldn't have come over, would he?

Just the same she spent the rest of the day in an agony of uncertainty. When it came to the time to get ready in the evening, her excitement was tempered by the fear of disappointment.

154

She showered and after slipping into filmy underwear put on the nylon pearl-buttoned dress which she had worn the day that Bruce had taken her to see Don Ignacio's garden. Her hair, freshly shampooed during the afternoon, swung silkily round her face. A touch of make-up on, and tanned legs slim in gold strapped sandals, she finished off with a dab of perfume. It was good to feel essentially feminine again after wearing nothing but old clothes for the past couple of weeks.

Just after dark, the cars belonging to the friends of the Fords began to converge along the track prior to starting out for the fiesta. Janet's heart spiralled down into her shoes when she went across the terrace with her mother and found a long white estate car filled with laughing partygoers, waiting to pick them up. However, she joined in the gaiety on the journey, reminding herself that Bruce was a busy man and could be held up in any number of places.

The *pueblo*, when they arrived, was already humming with activity and the festivities well under way. Fireworks exploded into multi-coloured lights in the sky and everyone was out in the garlanded streets, from the oldest of grandmothers in their best black dresses, to the tiniest of tots in colourful local costume. Tourists who had come to see the sights mingled happily with the villagers along the streets.

The Fords' party drove to the main *plaza* and parked their cars under the trees at the side. The centre of the square was dominated by a wooden-floored dance enclosure in which a group of young musicians hammered out a non-stop beat for the benefit of gyrating teenagers. There would later be a display of local dancing, a special attraction laid on for the tourists.

The square was lined with chairs, and there were the usual village cafés. The villa party made for the one where forms and tables had been set out under the loggia entrance. Mingling with the fragrance of the chestnut trees, cooling off after the heat of the day, was the heavier one of jasmine which climbed over the loggia above the tables.

Janet felt too on edge to sit down. She found a place at the end of the café enclosure beside the trees, to watch the goings-on in the square. Her mother, shrouded in the muted glow of the tiny coloured lights, was sitting chatting happily with Mrs Ford and one or two other feminine members of the party, while the men were giving their verdict on the local wine.

Francisco was in the group. Janet was used to seeing him on odd occasions when he drove in or out of the villa, and they always waved to each other as they passed. But though they were as friendly as ever, the closer companionship they had known in the early days of the summer was now a thing of the past.

He came to join her half an hour or so after they had arrived. Very proudly he told her that Santa Margarita was his native village. He knew everyone in the square, and almost every other one was a relative of his. Practically all of those who jostled by the front of the café shouted him a friendly greeting. He was enjoying his night amongst his own people. He left her after a while to join a group who were making for the floodlit dance area.

Janet watched him go, smiling over the hollowness inside her. She knew she didn't make very good company tonight. Standing at the edge of the villa group, she was supposed to be joining them in watching the fun in the square, but her gaze was trained more towards the shadows under the trees, where the cars were parked.

She was beginning to think that disappointment was going to be her companion tonight. Then, when the exhibition dancing had just started, she saw it—a dark polished shape sliding in amongst the shadows, the white-walled tyres striking through the darkness to make her pulses race.

No one, perhaps, but her took any notice of the gentle slam of a car door, swallowed up amidst the sound of flutes and guitars and tambourines, or of the lean figure picked out in pale suit making his way across to the café.

156

Janet's eyes following Bruce as he passed the table enclosure were starlit. Every line of his tanned features, the brilliant contrast of his cream shirt, his white smile as he acknowledged the Fords, were all stamped indelibly on her heart.

She watched him as he stood chatting in the group and took a sip of the drink he was handed, but when in the dim glow of the café lights he started to make his way in her direction, she swung her gaze wildly out to the square, her heart thumping madly.

She knew Bruce was behind her when her breathing became uneven. Or perhaps it was his close proximity which cut it off almost completely. She could hear the thudding of her pulses inside her head, and thought her knees were going to let her down. Then his arm came up to curve around her waist. He drew her gently against him, and rapturously, blissfully she relaxed.

Though they were outwardly watching the dancing display, Janet's gaze was too radiant to see anything but her own happiness. She doubted whether much of Bruce's attention was directed that way either, for his lips were dangerously close to her hair.

After a few minutes he said softly against her ear, 'There's a good hotel not far from here. Shall we go?'

Janet nodded against him. He guided her alongside him into the shadows. They disappeared by a side opening out of the loggia, and leaving the music and the gay life in the *plaza* they crossed silently to the car under the trees. In a few minutes they were cruising out into the black night and the countryside, leaving the lights of Santa Margarita behind them.

The tyres whispered over the road. Soon other lights were showing faintly in the distance. As they approached, one could make out the pale line of a beach and the lacy edge of black waves rustling in with a sigh on the still night air.

The hotel was a new white building. Bruce drove into the

car park. From here he guided Janet through to where couples were moving around to the strains of music on an open terrace. Soft lights from the doors were reflected in the tiles at the dancers' feet. Waiters floated discreetly between the arbour-sheltered tables.

It was a scene typical of any luxury hotel on a holiday island. Janet was stirred by the beauty of the view. Flowering shrubbery and trees beyond the tables were silhouetted against a backcloth of luminescent sky studded with stars. Bruce wasn't looking at the view. Without preamble he drew Janet into his arms and guided her on to the dance floor. Close against him, she thought she would burst with happiness.

She moved as though she had been dancing a lifetime with him. But this was mainly because he attempted nothing apart from drifting around with his head close to hers.

She lost all idea of time. When Bruce guided her towards the shadows of the trees, she didn't know whether she had been dancing five minutes or longer. He turned an arm about her waist as they walked to where they could hear the sea on the beach. With only the stars for company they stood before a bower of blossom which framed the night. In the silence she could hear his breathing, feel the warmth of it on her cheek. His arms curving about her, he drew her against him. His lips came down to meet hers.

There was nothing of the roughness of that first meadow kiss in his embrace, only a gentleness, a tenderness which melted her bones.

From her lips he trailed his mouth through her hair and across her throat. Drowning in the aching sweetness of his touch, she was far away, lost in an enchanted world, when he said deeply against her, 'We'd better be making our way back. The others will be getting ready for leaving.'

Janet nodded reluctantly and with shining eyes allowed him to lead her out through the hotel grounds and into the car.

She knew nothing of the ride back to Santa Margarita. She was lost to everything but the feel of Bruce beside her; his pale-suited shoulders alongside hers, his slim hands, immaculate shirt cuffs and heavy cuff-links at the wrist, swinging the wheel effortlessly.

The *pueblo*, when they got back, was still thick with people. The fireworks and the festivities would go on until two or three o'clock in the morning, but as Bruce had forecast, the villa party were on the point of getting ready to leave. Apparently the crowd had split up into groups to do different things, after the dancing display, so it was unlikely, Janet thought, that either she or Bruce had been missed.

Everyone was converging at the café as they left the car and strolled back through the shadows to join the throng. There was a slight commotion because Ralph Ford had mislaid the flash equipment belonging to his camera.

Bruce drifted in to give him a hand to locate it. Janet was swooped down on by her mother and a couple of pleasant-faced women around her mother's age, whose acquaintance they had made in the car on the journey out. They were all full of the experience they had had in a *bodega* just round the corner. Barrels as big as houses lined the walls, they said, and the wine gushed out of taps as freely as water, half of it running away along the gutter beneath, as the villagers' *botijas* overflowed.

In the move towards the cars it was taken for granted that Janet would travel back with the party she came out with. Stepping into the white estate car, she look around for Bruce. Francisco had several friends he wanted to give lifts to. As his car was small, Bruce was obligingly taking the overflow.

Happily Janet took her seat and settled down amidst the twittering excitement of her mother and her friends. Though she gave the appearance of listening to their chat on the drive back, nothing really penetrated the rosy glow

159

she was wrapped in. Dreamily, all she could think of was Bruce's arms around her, his lips on hers.

Janet awoke the next morning to the realisation that it was her mother's shopping day in Ibiza town. She couldn't think of anything less likely to coincide with her rapturous mood than browsing around the fish market or searching out the choicest vegetables. But she knew her mother enjoyed her company on that one afternoon a week. Also there was the thought that she needed assistance with the shopping bags.

They discussed what they would wear at the breakfast table. With September just around the corner the days were less inclined to be sticky. There was the merest suggestion of a lightness in the air, after months of languorous heat.

Mid-morning Janet took Dale for a walk, as she always did on shopping days, so that he would be pleasantly tired and ready to sleep indoors throughout the afternoon. Huge dragonflies zipped about at the bottom of the meadow. The grapes in the vine-fields down by the farm hung in huge lilac clusters. Soon they would turn black and succulent in the sun. Then they would be ready for picking.

Mrs Kendall made a salad for lunch. They rested in their own bedrooms for a while afterwards, then when they had washed and changed, and with shopping bags in hand, they locked up the house and set out to catch the bus into town.

Janet's heart gave a lilt when she saw Bruce's car across the track at the side gates. He must be working at the villa this afternoon. She would have liked to dawdle in case he took it into his mind, on the spur of the moment, to come over to the house. But they had already cut themselves fine for time. She was compelled to hurry off up the farm road alongside her mother in case they missed the bus.

The town was packed with its usual contingent of holidaymakers, plus a steamer-load of day trippers who had sailed in from a neighbouring island. Luckily they didn't get into the food markets much. All the same it was hard going, battling against the intrepid island women, who knew a bargain when they saw it, and weren't afraid to shout anyone down to get it.

When all the items on Mrs Kendall's list had been crossed off, mother and daughter sank down thankfully at a pavement café and refreshed themselves with coffee, and the pastries which were a speciality of the island. It was pleasant sitting in the shade watching the passers-by.

Feeling deliciously lazy, they stayed on sipping a second cup of coffee until it was time to catch the bus back to San Gabrielle. It left town at six-thirty. They got back to the village around seven-fifteen. As she stepped down at the top of the farm road, Janet sniffed the air appreciatively. After the rush and push of town, the blare of traffic, and the acrid smell of exhaust fumes, it was always good to get back to the peace and freshness of the countryside.

There was the softness of dusk in the air. The almond trees without a breath of breeze to stir them, stood etched against the red earth landscape, and dark blue mountains. From somewhere nearby came the trilling musical note of a nightbird.

Even with the heavy shopping bags to carry, the walk down the farm road to the house was a pleasure. As they made their way up the railway track to the terrace they could hear Dale excitedly barking at their approaching footsteps. Janet hurried to let him out, and laughed as he tore in wide circles all over the garden, rushing back every few minutes to reassure himself that they really had arrived by nuzzling his nose into their hands, then hurling himself delightedly back at the fig trees.

Janet left him to wear himself out, and went to help her mother unpack the shopping. When everything was tidied away they went out to sit on the patio to get their breath back. Soon they would start to prepare a late meal, but first it was soothing to sit with a relaxing drink and watch the changing colours of the gathering dusk.

The sky had darkened to an unbelievably brilliant turquoise blue and was slashed dramatically with plumes of even more brilliant salmon pink, when the phut-phut sound of a light motor-cycle coming down the farm road took their attention out to the end of the track. It was always interesting to see who was passing.

Someimes it was Pablo the shepherd, on his way to the farm to start work. During the summer months the sheep had to be taken out to graze through the night, for they would never have survived a day in the heat. Sometimes it was the electricity man in his uniform going down to collect his dues. Although he wasn't likely to be going to the farm at this time of night.

As it happened it *was* a man in uniform on a dusty red motorised bike, and surprisingly he turned in on to the railway track and bumped his way precariously up to the house. As he came nearer Janet recognised him as the clerk who worked behind the counter at the town hall. He looked hot and not a little put out as he dismounted and stood his machine up.

Rising from her chair Janet explained to her mother that he was from the *ayuntamiento* and Mrs Kendall, always hospitable, hurried to invite him inside for a drink and a sit down.

He declined the *cerveza*, the bottled beer which she kept in the fridge for the *butano* men. He agreed to come inside, though not to sit down. Apparently he had brought a message from the town hall. He had called once this afternoon, but they had been out, so he had been obliged to make this second trip. He had just finished work, and was anxious to get home.

All this Janet gathered in a few moments. Her long stay on the island, plus her frequent visits to the village, had given her a reasonable understanding of the language. She listened carefully now to what the clerk had to say.

Occasionally she tilted her head when she didn't quite

get a word. Once or twice she smiled at his remarks, and nodded to show that everything was quite clear. Then, his work finished, the *ayuntamiento* official bade them both a polite '*Buenas noches*' and left to chug away on his spluttering transport.

Mrs Kendall, whose Spanish never got any further than a couple of dozen words, had lost interest in trying to fathom the conversation and had drifted into arranging a bowl of fruit on the table. When the sound of the bicycle had faded she asked absently over her shoulder, 'Was it anything important, dear?'

'Fairly,' Janet said lightly. She didn't give anything away at once, but floated around teasingly.

Her mother looked at her. Her curiosity growing, she asked laughingly, 'What did the man come for?'

'Well,' Janet savoured the moment, then went on with a rush, 'the town hall have heard from Madrid at last about the disused railway track. It seems that they have no authority to parcel it out themselves.'

Mrs Kendall shrugged good-naturedly. 'So what complications have we got now?' she sighed, turning back to arrange the fruit bowl.

'That's just it. There *are* no complications.' Janet reclaimed her attention. 'Apparently anyone can now buy what they like provided they deal personally with the capital.'

Her mother digested this, and repeated it as she understood it. 'You mean all they have to do is to go there and they get what they want?'

'If it's government land and it's for sale, yes,' Janet nodded.

She saw her mother's gaze leave hers and travel out beyond the living room window. As it came to rest significantly on the dark polished car waiting outside the villa gates, Mrs Kendall said, 'So whoever gets to Madrid first gets the track.'

'Bruce wouldn't go ahead of us,' Janet laughed radiantly, the memory of his lips on hers a warm glow in her mind. 'He knows we can't afford to employ a lawyer. And even if we had the fare *I* wouldn't know what to do.'

Mrs Kendall agreed with that. Her attention was already beginning to wander towards thoughts of supper. Moving in the direction of the kitchen, she asked, half her mind on the *gambas*, the large prawns they had bought in the fish market, 'What do you think would be the best way to act, then, Jan?'

'We won't do anything until I've seen Bruce,' said Janet, following her mother into the kitchen. 'He might have been over this afternoon while we were out, so we'll probably have to wait until tomorrow.'

After supper they listened to the English radio while Mrs Kendall did some crocheting on the toddler's dress she had started. But both were tired after their day, and when Janet returned after taking Dale down the meadow a little way beneath the stars, they locked up the house, glad to have an early night.

The following morning Janet kept an eye on Bruce's car while she dusted in the living room. He would be busy in his office in the villa this morning, but she would see him when he came out to drive to town some time this afternoon.

Her mother went off for her siesta after lunch. Janet sat and rocked desultorily in her chair on the patio, listening for a footfall on the villa steps. She went inside during the drowsy afternoon to revive herself with a drink.

Later, out again on the patio, she was surprised to see that the time had crept round to four o'clock. Bruce wouldn't be going to town at this time of day. It was almost the hour when, normally, he was preparing to drive back.

Rising from her chair, she wandered out on to the terrace wondering what she ought to do. She hadn't the nerve to go up the villa steps looking for him. He might be in conference in the grounds with Ralph Ford, and then she wouldn't know where to put herself.

But she could wander out past the front gates. If he was strolling there, or she could catch sight of him on his own ...

She went back inside and unhooked the lead from behind the door and, on the pretext of taking the dog for a walk, started out down the track. Dale, delighted at this unexpected treat, tugged excitedly, his short little legs straddling over the uneven surface in his eagerness to get wherever he thought they were going. Out on the farm road, however, the brilliant glare slowed him down and after a while he was content to sniff leisurely in the undergrowth at the sides.

Janet dawdled past the villa gates. Though she waited, allowing Dale to take as long as he liked on the walk by, she saw nothing, mainly because the Fords' big expensive American car, which was parked in the inky shade of overhanging greenery, somewhat obstructed the view. She went right on up to the carob tree beside the main road, because she hadn't the heart to cheat Dale out of his walk, then she turned back.

It was beginning to look as though she had come out on a fruitless trip when half way down the farm road she heard the sound of a car starting up. Her heart lifting, she hurried. Soon she saw that it was Francisco's car which had been making the noise. As she approached the villa entrance it came weaving its way out slowly through the gates.

She waved gaily in reply to Francisco's salute. Then as he was about to drive off she thought to call after him. 'I've been waiting to have a word with Bruce. Is he very busy today?'

'Bruce?' Francisco was on the point of speeding away. He threw over his shoulder in passing, 'He's in Madrid.'

Madrid! Janet turned to stone where she stood.

'I drove him to the airport yesterday afternoon,' Francisco called back, smiling, not knowing that he was cutting off her life's blood.

Yesterday! The day they had heard about the track.

'Thanks!' Janet waved after him with a ghastly smile and turned back towards the house.

She didn't know how she managed to cover the distance still on her feet. She felt as though she had been hit by a runaway boulder.

Indoors, her mother, floating around in a cotton kimono after her nap, was routing out a lemon from the fruit bowl for the afternoon tea. She looked at Janet as she came in and smiled absently. 'Hello, dear. Have you been out?'

Janet followed her into the kitchen. She didn't bother to explain where she had been. She said in strained tones from white marble-like features, 'Bruce is in Madrid.' And as her mother lifted her head quickly from the knife she was using, Janet added quiveringly, 'He's gone to buy the track for the Fords.'

She could do nothing then except stumble away blindly to her room. She locked the door behind her and flung herself on the bed.

She stayed there until it grew dark, hearing the cicadas strike up their clamour in the meadow. A little later her mother knocked at the door brightly. 'Janet! Supper's ready.' And in worried coaxing tones, 'Do come out, dear, and try something to eat.'

Janet rose and dragged over to the mirror to tidy her hair. Her body felt like lead. With an effort she made her way to the kitchen.

Mrs Kendall had put a vase of fresh flowers on the table. Also she had searched out gay table napkins and her best glassware. Though she tried to appear in the best of spirits as she chatted away about all the cooking she had done, sympathy and compassion were written all over the face she turned to her daughter.

They sat down in silence and started to eat. After a while

166

Mrs Kendall, trying to be a help, ventured to point out, 'Well, Bruce has his job to do, I suppose, and . . .'

'Oh, Mother!' Janet choked back a sob while she tried to eat. 'Please don't talk about it.'

Mrs Kendall made no more comments. They finished the rest of the meal in weighty silence. They washed up, then sat in the living room winding wool into balls. Mrs Kendall had plenty of other jobs to do, but she wanted something where she could draw her daughter in with her work.

Janet sat with a lack-lustre gaze and watched the strand of wool travel from right to left as the skein grew less on her hands. She could think of nothing but this afternoon's bombshell. She ought to have guessed it would happen, of course. But she had been so sure that Bruce would come across to the house to talk things over. Her mother knew human nature better than she did. One of her first thoughts had been that Bruce might go to Madrid ahead of them.

Around ten o'clock Dale came to sit up and look his most appealing, which was his way of asking her for his evening walk. It was useless to tell him that she had heart for nothing. She got his lead and let him tug her down the meadow and back. It was a relief after that to get to bed and lie alone with her misery in the darkness.

The following morning, for her mother's sake, she rose and tried to act as though it was a normal day. In cotton housecoat she joined her for breakfast on the side terrace with its view of the mountains, and made an effort to appear interested as they discussed the day's activities.

Mrs Kendall thought it would be a good idea to do some tidying up at the bottom of the meadow. Throughout the summer months things had been rather let go down there. The area around the chicken run was hopelessly choked with dried grass and weeds and the goat paddock needed drastically clearing. Janet agreed slackly that they ought to do something about it.

As soon as the normal household tasks were completed

they put on their oldest clothes and started out down the path. Dale, of course, was in his element. He could trot around to his heart's content down there and he had all the shade he needed under the big old almond tree.

They worked with hand scythes, secateurs, and various tools from the old shed until lunch-time, when Mrs Kendall got the idea of bringing a picnic basket down. Janet washed her hands in cool water from the well and sat down to grilled sardines, stuffed olives, and fruit yoghourt. Though she found it difficult to get anything down her constricted throat, she forced a smile and complimented her mother on the meal, because she knew how hard she was trying to cheer her up.

They worked through the afternoon hacking at old thistles and brambles until the chicken run was in an airy open space again, and the goat compound sweet and green in the shade.

It was approaching six o'clock when they had piled the last of the refuse in a far corner to be burned at a later date. They put the tools back in the shed and trudged up the path to the house.

Mrs Kendall went straight off for a shower and a lie-down. Janet watched her go with a wan, tender smile. She knew her mother had purposely planned a day full of hard work to take her mind off other things. She was grateful to her, and all in favour of the remedy. Though she was worn out now she daren't stop. The wearier she got the less inclination she would have to think.

She washed and put on a cool cotton dress and went off to the kitchen. Here, taking her time, she cooked a three-course meal for the two of them. She set out the long polished table in the living room and served it in the red glow from the lamps.

She wouldn't let her mother assist with the washing up afterwards, but completed the chore herself. In addition she gave the kitchen an extra going over. When her work was finished she noticed thankfully that Dale, having been out all day, was sprawled in his basket with no thoughts of an evening walk. She kissed her mother goodnight, went to clean up under the shower, then fell into bed, too exhausted to do anything but sleep.

The following morning brought a small surprise. Miguel, the leather-faced old man from the farm, stopped his cart at the end of the track and came trudging up with something in a bundle. It turned out to be a kitten so tiny it fitted in the palm of Mrs Kendall's hand. She was delighted with it. It had practically the same colouring and markings as the cat she had lost, and she promptly named it Twiggy again. Janet was sure it would never be as lovable as Twiggy number one. Still, she rubbed her cheek against its soft fur and gazed into its china blue eyes.

When Miguel had tossed back a glass of wine as though it was water, he told them he was going into San Gabrielle and asked them if there was anything they wanted. It occurred to Mrs Kendall that he might pick up the mail. Janet hadn't been into the village for two or three days so it was possible there might be letters waiting at the shop. Miguel told them he would drop anything in on his way past back to the farm in the afternoon.

Janet returned to the pile of washing she had started in the back. Her mother went off to search out a box for the new Twiggy.

The day was warm without being too enervating. In light sun-dresses they lunched out on the side terrace in the shade. Afterwards Janet ironed all she had washed, practically the whole of her wardrobe. She was folding everything in the kitchen ready for transferring through to her bedroom, when a shout came from the farm road.

Miguel, whom they had forgotten all about, was waving a sheaf of letters in his hand at the end of the garden. Obviously anxious to get back to the farm for a meal and his siesta, he didn't want to be bothered getting down from

169

the cart.

'I'll go,' said Mrs Kendall, leaving Janet to get on with her work.

She had hung most of her clothes back in the wardrobe when her mother returned, with three or four letters in her hand. One of these she gave to Janet, but her mind didn't seem to be on what it was doing. Her kindly animated features were dulled by a certain seriousness. She watched Janet as she told her, 'Bruce is back. I saw him just now getting out of a taxi at the villa gates.'

Janet tensed. She was suddenly at a loss where to run to. She went blindly into the garden to gather her thoughts, thinking she had all afternoon to decide what to do. Pacing, white-faced, she lifted her head after a few moments and was startled to see Bruce coming across the track from the villa side entrance. He must have stayed only long enough to drop his luggage before making his way through the grounds to the steps opposite the house.

She stumbled across the garden. She had no wish to be seen. She got to the patio and had disappeared indoors when he surprised her by coming in at the back.

She swayed into the living room to meet him entering at the other end. They faced each other across the length of the room. Her mother stayed discreetly out of the way.

For a moment Janet's heart dipped when she saw how tired Bruce looked. His face was pale and travel-worn. He hadn't even allowed himself time for a proper shave. Quickly she hardened herself against these kind of feelings. Why should she care if he had chosen to work himself to a standstill during the whole of the two days he had been gone, simply to further his own ends?

The thought made her anger claw at her insides like a pain. It gave her voice a queer high-pitched sound and made her smile look brittle and pasted on. She hadn't planned to give him any of her time, but since the confrontation had been forced on her, she quivered at him, 'Did you enjoy

170

your trip?'

'Passably.'

She ignored the worn look about his smile and piped acidly, 'I thought you might.'

His blue gaze fixed on her, he said, 'I've just got back. I came straight over.'

'Well, I wish you hadn't,' she choked, finding that she couldn't keep up as well as she would have liked. As she swung away to blink back a tear, Bruce took a step forward.

'Now wait a minute,' he said harshly.

'What is there to wait for?' She flung back at him. 'So that you can crow about your trip to Madrid? I know why you went. You've bought the track for the villa, haven't you?'

'Yes.' His reply was calm and matter-of-fact.

Janet felt herself breaking up into small pieces. That was all she needed to hear. 'Well, thank you for telling me,' she managed shakily through a blaze of tears. 'Temporarily I'd forgotten you were a successful lawyer.' She made it clear that she was hinting at their moments together in the hotel garden. 'I ought to have known that you would allow nothing to come between you and your work.'

'Janet, listen to me!' His face white, Bruce moved towards her.

But Janet was unable to stem the flow of tears any longer. 'I've done all the listening I care to, thank you,' she said with a shaking voice. 'I never want to speak to you or see you again!'

She wouldn't let herself see his haggard look. There might have been something between them once, but that was all finished now. She would never, *never* forgive him for what he had done.

Eyes brimming, she ran to her room, and slamming and locking the door flung herself sobbing on to the bed.

CHAPTER TWELVE

MRS KENDALL sat in a chair and watched Janet fold the things from her wardrobe and pack them slowly into the open suitcases on the bed. Her amiable features dimmed by a look of despondency, she sighed, 'Do you *have* to go, dear?'

'Yes, Mother,' Janet nodded slackly. Her face was pale and there were violet smudges under her eyes. Folding her white nylon dress with a lump in her throat, she tried to smile as she went on, 'I've got a living to earn, remember. You've only got your pension. And there's really no need for me to stay now.'

'I suppose not, dear,' Mrs Kendall said gloomily.

'Besides,' Janet struggled to sound bright and practical, 'that letter you gave me yesterday was from Nona. She's got herself married. She's moved out of the flat and Angela left last week, so if I don't get back I'll have nowhere to live.'

'But you won't be able to keep a big place like that on your own.' Her mother's eyes widened.

'I'll have to get someone to share again,' Janet shrugged.

'What a business!' Mrs Kendall sighed. She watched Janet move around for a while, then said casually, 'I hear that Bruce has severed all his business ties with London. Rumour has it that he's working permanently in Ibiza with his main office in Madrid.'

Janet's face was wooden. She said bitterly, 'He should do well. Considering what he did for his last clients, the Fords.'

When it came to it, it was a wrench leaving the island.

172

Janet didn't realise how much it had all become a part of her; her mother's little house, the picturesque countryside, San Gabrielle on the hill with its placid, easy-going villagers. She was going to miss it all badly at first, living her sombre city life.

As though to make it all the harder to say goodbye, the September sky sparkled at its bluest on the day of her departure. The mountains ranged themselves conspiratorially in majestic splendour, their pine-clad foothills appearing almost close enough to touch.

Janet took Dale for a last walk down the meadow, a lump in her throat when she brought him back and hugged him close. The second Twiggy came in for a cuddle too, though she was far too young yet to know what life was all about.

Janet had booked a taxi to come out from the airport, so there was nothing to do but wait for its arrival. With her suitcases beside her on the terrace she began to have misgivings about leaving her mother. Reassuring herself for the hundredth time, she made the most of last-minute conversation and asked anxiously, 'Are you sure you're going to be all right? How will you manage without the drive?'

Her mother, putting on a happy face, said perkily, 'Oh, don't worry about me. I'll have a gate put in from the farm road and get the *butano* men to carry the gas up through the garden. They won't mind.'

Janet nodded and went straight on with, 'And you will phone me if you're feeling the teeniest bit unwell?'

'Now don't fuss, dear,' Mrs Kendall twinkled affectionately. 'You know I'm as strong as an ox. And I'll be over to see all my family as usual at Christmas.'

They jerked along in this way with similar oddments of chat until the taxi finally came round the corner of the villa and up the track. Janet's cases were humped into the boot. She hugged her mother for the last time and took her seat. The taxi turned slowly and crunched away.

Through a tear-starred gaze she waved at her mother,

who was dabbing her eyes, perhaps because things hadn't turned out as she would have liked them to, and at Dale, who had no idea that she wasn't coming back.

Out on the farm road she watched the villa fall away behind her. She could still see its red roof and huge black palms when they were well on the way to the village.

Turning at last, her throat painfully constricted, she slumped back in her seat, engulfed in misery.

On the coastal route to the airport she closed her heart to the views. Unless her mother urgently needed her she wouldn't be coming back to Ibiza.

Because she had made her plane seat reservation by phone it was necessary to get to the airport early to pick up her ticket. She hated the hanging about in the airport lounge. She would have liked to step straight into an aircraft which was about to take off, making her break with the island quick and less painful. As it was she was compelled to rub shoulders with noisy, laughing tourists, who, relaxed and sun-tanned after their holiday, were looking forward to the added excitement of flying back home.

The stewardesses hurried about their tasks with smiling faces. Members of the flight crews stood around or strolled through their various gates making jokes with each other. The whole world seemed gay and carefree. It was only she, Janet told herself, who sat alone in black despair.

At last her plane arrived and she was able to merge in with the stream of people making their way out to the airstrip. By the time she got on board the plane was fairly full. Owing to a trick of fate a stewardess found her a seat directly in front of the cream curtain which partitioned off the first-class area.

Her heart aching somewhere up in her throat, Janet wondered what kind of a person was sitting on the other side of the curtain. Would it be a keen-eyed, polished lawyer type with his briefcase opened before him, already immersed in his work? She got up once during the flight and caught a glimpse through the curtain. There was no one like that back there. Just a stout woman in a big black hat sipping coffee from a glass cup.

In an effort to cheer herself a little, she passed the time by imagining that this was actually the day that she was flying out to Ibiza, and Bruce really was sitting on the other side of the curtain. Though everything had turned out so disastrously, if she could have turned the calendar back to that day she knew she would have done.

When the plane touched down in England it was already growing dark. There were the Customs preliminaries to go through, then she was able to board a bus bound for the city centre. There was not much life about the streets. The shops were closed and only the lights from the odd café or cinema added a touch of colour to the night. Janet had chosen Sunday to travel so that she could get straight back to work on the following Monday morning.

She caught a taxi from the bus terminal. It seemed strange to see tall old buildings and cars sweeping to right and left, when she had grown accustomed to knowing only the lazy little town of Ibiza.

In the district where the flat was situated the lights were less frequent. She would have soon lost her bearings if the taxi driver hadn't been familiar with the area. He stopped at the front door with the flight of steps leading up to it. While she was searching for money to pay him, he carried her cases up for her. She gave him his tip and heard the car rumble away as she turned the key in the lock.

The smell of stale air and damp corners met her as she walked inside. In the hall she put her cases down and switched on the lights. Everywhere was grubby. Angela, the last to leave after living the past week or so on her own, hadn't been too particular, apparently.

The front room was thick with dust. Cigarette packets, biscuit wrappings, and scraps of this and that littered the fireplace and furniture. The kitchen reeked of sour milk bottles that had never been put out. The bathroom was passable, though the floor was peppered with face powder and odd hair-grips.

Depressed beyond measure, Janet looked into the bedroom that Angela had used and quickly closed the door on its unsightliness. Thankfully Nona's room was neat and tidy, except for the film of dust which had collected since her departure.

Mrs Kendall, using foresight, had packed her daughter enough groceries to see her over the weekend. Janet, removing everything from the bag she had carried as hand luggage, made herself a light snack, then switching all the lights off on the dismal scene she went to bed.

She rose early the next morning and caught the bus to work. Being a secretarial agency it was all very impersonal. She was assigned to a block of offices a few minutes' walk away and by ten o'clock was typing busily. There was no one to ask her about her trip to Ibiza, no one to comment on her paleness under her tan, or her violet-shadowed eyes. She was just a typist engaged to cope with excess work.

She ate out at lunch time and arriving back at the flat in the evening, ate out again, returning after a walk through the streets to go to bed. She dragged through each day in this way. She knew that sooner or later she was going to have to tackle the business of cleaning the flat. But despite the fact that the very place abhorred her as it was, she could find no incentive beneath the weight of her unhappiness to do anything about it.

On Thursday evening she took the tube out to see Nona. Her marriage had come as no surprise to Janet. Throughout the summer months her letters had been veering more and more in that direction. Then just recently, according to her friend's last communication, Robert, the man in question, had received promotion. Wasting no more time, they had got married on the strength of it, and put all their savings plus Nona's holiday money into buying a new flat in Bayswater. They hadn't had a honeymoon or a holiday yet, but they were hoping that would come the following year.

Janet found Bellevere Gardens, a neat little block of flats on a new road, a short way from the tube station. She went into the pleasantly lit foyer and took the lift to the flat number she had on the letter in her bag. It turned out to be the end one along a tiled corridor. A thin strip of light showed under the door. There was the sound of voices and an occasional ripple of laughter coming from within. She rang the bell loudly.

Almost at once the door was flung open and Nona stood there looking flushed and radiant, the frill of a red heart-shaped apron framing her face, a tea towel in her hand. 'Why, it's Janet!' she gasped, delighted, and grabbing her, 'Well, come on in!'

'Hello, Nona,' Janet smiled, blinking a little in the brightness. She entered a room filled with the new and shining things of newlyweds. The furniture gleamed like glass, the cushions hadn't had time to lose that shop window look. There were framed wedding photographs around and an ultra-modern electric fire shone a warm glow against the chill of the night.

Nona had tossed her tea towel into the kitchen and was leading Janet across the room to where a stolid-looking young man with fair curling hair sat with books spread before him at a table beside the curtained window. 'This is Janet, my old flatmate,' she said to him. 'You remember! I told you, she had to go out to her mother's to Ibiza.'

'I remember.' The young man rose to quite a height and with a grin took her hand in a bear grip. He gave her a wink and added, 'She used to talk about nothing else.'

'This is Robert,' Nona said shyly. 'He's got a bit of book work to do before morning.' She dropped a kiss lightly on his cheek as he sat down again and told him softly, 'We won't disturb you, love.'

'It's nice to know you, Robert,' Janet smiled before they

moved away.

'Would you like to see the flat?' Nona asked proudly. She began to guide Janet around. 'This is the kitchen.' She switched the light on in a spruce little area done out entirely in white, with lime green fittings. 'The bathroom's along here.'

She led her along a passageway out of the living room, to peep in on coffee-coloured tiles and matching porcelain fittings.

'This is the main bedroom.' They wandered across and in over a deep red carpet to where curtains hung frothily at the windows, matching perfectly with the organdie fitted bedspread.

'And that's as far as we've got with the furnishings,' Nona laughed ruefully. 'Oh, there's a balcony out here,' she opened the door on a little stone built enclosure, 'and there's one at the front.'

Janet looked around her appreciatively, admiring the smart little dressing table and roomy wardrobe. 'You've certainly got a lovely place here, Nona,' she remarked sincerely.

Nona moved around happily, at the same time admitting with a wry look, 'Oh, we'll be paying out most of our wages for the next couple of years and heaven knows how much longer, with the mortgage. But it's wonderful to have a home of your own.'

'I can see you love it,' Janet twinkled, musing over her friend's pretty apron and flushed look.

'Me?' Nona laughed at herself. 'I'm an old hand now. I've been married almost four weeks.' She stopped suddenly, possibly because her perceptive gaze had noticed for the first time Janet's washed-out look.

Stepping down from her high-flying cloud, she scolded herself with, 'But here's me going on about myself. How *are* you?' She dropped down on the quilted commode at the end of the bed and patted the seat beside her. 'How was

Ibiza?'

Janet grimaced a smile, strolling to join her. 'London doesn't compare very well at the moment,' she confessed.

'Did you get the track?' her friend asked cheerily.

'No.' Janet shook her head.

'Bad luck!' Nona was genuinely sympathetic. 'What happened?'

'Oh, the villa people had a lawyer working for them.' Janet tried to shrug lightly. 'He was much too clever for Mother and me.'

Nona didn't miss the despondency behind the reply. Discerning enough to link it with the stricken look she had noticed beneath her friend's calm exterior, she was silent for a moment before saying casually, 'A legal mind, eh?' She bent to pick an imaginary piece of fluff off her slipper. 'Was he married?'

'No,' Janet replied.

'What was he like?' Nona kept her voice casual.

'Bruce? Oh, tallish . . . slim . . .' Janet tried to sound off-hand over the pain in her throat. How could she say that he had eyes as fathomless and blue as Ibizan skies? That the charm of his smile when he directed it your way could hit you behind the knees. That she loved him as she would never love a man again. And that he had betrayed her.

As she was looking down at her shoes, a voice came from along the hallway, 'All right, girls, you can come out now. I've finished.'

Nona got up smiling at her husband's voice. 'Good, we can go and sit by the fire.' She led the way out.

In the living room Robert was rubbing his hands pleased with himself. 'Right! Now who's for a nice cup of coffee?' he asked as they entered.

'Well, as I've just got rid of the last lot of washing up, *you* can have a bash,' Nona retorted playfully.

'My pleasure.' He bowed teasingly. 'And you're a rotten hostess anyway. You haven't even asked Janet to take her coat off.'

Laughingly, as the couple larked about with each other, Janet unbuttoned her coat and had it taken from her and hung on a hook.

While Robert worked noisily in the kitchen, eager to show off his prowess in that department, Janet and Nona took the armchairs beside the fire.

'What was the flat like when you got back?' Nona asked when they were settled.

'Pretty ropey,' Janet said wryly. 'Still is. I haven't got round to cleaning it up yet.'

Her reply seemed to be only what Nona expected. 'Angela was impossible,' she sighed, and not without a trace of humour. 'It always amazed me how she could go out and model those beautiful gowns with that stately, queenly look of hers, and then come back and eat steak and chips in bed.'

'Come to think of it, I think I did see a plate and a knife and fork on the bedside table,' Janet said, joining in her amusement.

'Have you got anyone to share with you yet?' her friend asked.

'No. I've lost contact with most of the typists I knew. I expect I'll have to advertise, though I can't say I fancy the idea of taking in a total stranger.' Janet gave a gleam of humour again. 'She might be worse than Angela.'

Nona was deep in thought. 'Look,' she said suddenly, 'why don't you come and live here for a while? We've got a spare room with a bed and a cupboard in it.'

'Oh, I couldn't do that,' Janet smiled, taken aback. 'Though thank you for offering.'

'Well, why not?' Nona persisted, warming to the idea. 'It will give you time to sort yourself out. You can look around at your leisure for something nicer than that old place, and if you have to share, at least it will give you breathing space, to choose someone you can get along with.'

180

'It's sweet of you to suggest it, Nona,' Janet said gratefully, 'but no.'

Nona sighed, then begged for help from the kitchen. 'Robert, talk some sense into her.'

Her husband came out with the coffee percolator in his hand, having heard every word. 'I think she's right, Janet,' he said with a seriousness around his grin. 'I've been to the old flat once or twice. Personally I think you're best out of it.' Seeing that she still hesitated, he added, 'You'd actually be doing us a favour. I'll have to work over quite a bit these next few weeks doing the Christmas displays. You'd be company for Nona in the evenings.'

Put like that, Janet gave it some thought. She had to admit that the idea of going back to the old flat each night appalled her. Perhaps it might be as well to make a complete break with the old life and start up anew somewhere. She could give Nona the money she normally paid for her rent until she found something. She knew she would have a job to get her to take it, but she would insist. And at least it would be a help towards their hire-purchase payments. They were on the phone, so she could keep in touch with her mother.

Giving it careful consideration, she said at last with a dubious smile, 'If you're sure I won't be a nuisance. I'll come and stay, just for a week or two.'

'Sensible girl,' Robert nodded, and returned to his kitchen.

Nona looked pleased at having done something to lift her friend's spirits a little. 'I'll come and help you with your flat-hunting,' she said cheerfully. 'We'll find you something really nice. Now,' she went off on a thinking bout again, 'what day is it? Thursday. Mmmm, I'm working late tomorrow night, but I've only my shopping to do on Saturday. Tell you what,' she suggested brightly, 'I'll come round about tea time on Saturday and we'll clean the flat through together. Robert can easily borrow a van from the store to pick up your stuff, when he's finished.'

'Oh, that's awfully nice of you,' Janet protested. 'But you don't have to help me clean up the flat. Really!'

'Why shouldn't I?' Nona bulldozed aside her arguments. 'It's just as much my responsibility as yours. I used to live there, remember?'

Seeing that she was determined to be of some assistance Janet capitulated with a smile and assented to the arrangements.

The coffee arrived and the three of them sat chatting over various topics, until Janet decided it was time for her to leave. She would have been quite happy to walk to the tube station on her own, but the couple insisted on accompanying her. And so they strolled, Robert with his arm around his wife's waist, along the lamplit streets, coats buttoned against the keen night air.

Leaving the pair to catch her train, Janet walked down the steps to the underground, her eyes glistened at the overpowering force of Nona's happiness. She knew how she felt. She had known a brief taste of that heaven herself once. The one difference was that hers was a love destined from the start never to work out. She swallowed back her misery. That was life, she supposed. Not everyone ended up happily ever after.

As the train rattled on its way below ground she sat staring out into the nothingness over the rawness inside her. It was almost a week now since she had left Ibiza. What would it be like in two weeks? A month? A year? Would she be feeling like this in twenty years' time?

Janet contrived to work over on Saturday afternoon answering someone's cry for a rush typing job, so that when she arrived at the flat Nona practically followed her in on her heels. Rain was falling steadily from a dull gunmetal grey sky—a fitting accompaniment, they grimaced, for their dismal task.

182

They had a light snack to cheer themselves, then set to work. Janet had packed all her possessions the night before. With her cases and boxes standing in the hall there was nothing to do except take each room in turn and dust it and sweep and generally clear out excess rubbish.

Janet noticed that the task was nowhere near as overwhelming with Nona's willing presence. They got through the rooms quickly, leaving the kitchen until last because it was in the worst state.

There was the hall to do, and as it was fast growing dark Janet went to switch on the light. Nothing happened. 'This bulb must have gone,' she remarked casually. 'I'll have to try and manage without it.'

Nona, coming out of one of the bedrooms, flicked the switch on there. She went on flicking. 'That's funny, there's no light here either.' She went round all the rooms with the same result and came back to look blankly at Janet. 'There's no electricity.' She lapsed thoughtful for a moment, then said suddenly, 'I wonder if that scatterbrain Angela paid the bill? I left the money for her on top of the old biscuit tin in the kitchen.'

They rushed to find out, and sure enough the notes were still in the envelope gathering dust on the kitchen cabinet.

'That girl!' Nona expostulated. 'I told her half a dozen times not to forget to pay it.'

'The landlord must have let the man in this morning to turn the electricity off,' Janet surmised. 'It was on last night.'

They stood around in the gathering gloom until Nona shrugged philosophically, 'Oh well, we've practically finished anyway. There's some tatty candles round here somewhere. Been here for years. We can get enough light from them to tidy up the kitchen.'

They searched around and found a packet of half a dozen bent, yellowing candles in a cupboard under the sink. They lit two and stood them in the front room. The other four

183

gave sufficient glow to allow them to do a reasonable job in the kitchen.

They had whittled the tasks down to the last one of washing up the bits and pieces gathered on their purge of the rooms when the phone rang.

Its harsh sound dropped like a bolt on the silence, making them both jump almost into each other's arms in the gloom.

'I'll get it,' Janet said, groping her way along the hall. She didn't know why, but she had a feeling it was her mother calling. She always waited for the cheaper rate in the evening to ring, and this would just be about her time.

She picked up the receiver. There was a knot of apprehension in her stomach when she heard the familiar tones coming over the line. 'Mother?' she asked worriedly. 'Are you all right?'

'All right, dear? Why, yes, I never felt better.' Her laughter sounded clear.

There was something much more than just the usual animation in her voice as she prattled, 'Oh, Jan, I wish you'd been here this week. The things that have been happening! The whole length of the track has been levelled and tarmacked and walled in as part of my meadow and garden. I've got one of those lovely Spanish overhanging gateways at the front. They asked me if I wanted to give the house a name so that they could hang it over the drive. I thought of *Casa Content*. Do you like that, Jan? I think it's got a nice ring to it . . .'

'Mother, I'm not with you.' Janet pulled her up, dazed and confused. 'Are you saying that the track is yours . . . ? I don't understand . . . How can it be when it was bought for the villa?'

'Well, that's just it, dear,' Mrs Kendall explained confidingly. 'It *was* bought for the villa. But guess who owns it? I thought it was the Fords, but it turns out that they were only renting it for the summer.' She waited a moment to give spice to her words, before she added, 'It's Bruce's property!' And on a ripple of laughter, 'So naturally he can do what he likes with it. He must have known when he went to see about the business of buying the track of course, what he was going to do ... but, my dear, who would have thought ... ! I'm sure *I* never suspected ...'

'Wait a minute.' Janet cut across her mother's chatter, feeling faint. 'I have to get this straight ... Are you trying to tell me that Bruce has owned the villa all the time, and that he went to Madrid for the sole purpose of turning the track over to us?'

'Yes,' Mrs Kendall admitted in a word, then she bubbled on again, 'He wouldn't let me tell you until everything was finished ... he flew out this afternoon. I only ...'

'I can't believe it! Nothing makes sense ...' Janet began to gabble, dreamily competing with the stream of talk coming over the phone. Though her eyes shone she was too stunned to make anything but incoherent remarks while her mind tried to grapple with the one beautiful, blinding, heart-soaring realisation. Bruce hadn't betrayed her after all.

In the midst of them both talking across one another, with neither listening, the door bell rang. Janet was startled almost as badly as she had been when the phone had rung. Everything was happening tonight. Her breath cutting off in her throat at a sudden wild thought, she said in strangled tones over the wire, 'Mother, the door bell's ringing ...'

'Oh well, dear, I'm going now,' Mrs Kendall chuckled down the ear-piece. 'I just wanted to let you know. 'Bye, Jan!' Promptly she rang off.

Janet's hands trembled as she hung up. Though she was terrified of going to the door she couldn't keep herself away.

Battling with all kinds of conflicting emotions, she opened up. A lean shape looking slightly unfamiliar in white raincoat and trilby danced before the dazzle in her eyes. Her senses bursting into stars of joy she fell into the open arms. 'Bruce!'

The kiss was long and satisfying. When she could bring herself to, Janet drew away to look at him. His face, in the light of the street lamp, was thinner. There was a strand or two of grey in the dark hair under his hat. Her soft gaze on him, he gleamed ironically, 'Can I come in? It's raining.'

Janet laughed and stepped inside with him. To hide her starry-eyed confusion she said, 'Mother just phoned.'

Nona was in the hall, the candle in her hand lighting up her rather quixotic smile. 'I thought I'd better come along and see who was ringing the door bell,' she said, twinkling.

'This is Bruce,' Janet said shyly. And to him, 'This is Nona, my flatmate.' She explained the candle lamely, 'The electricity's been cut off.'

'Hello, Nona.' Bruce gave her one of his rare white smiles, unbuttoning his raincoat. To Janet he moved towards the front room as though he had been entering candle lit interiors all his life and asked, 'Can we go in here?'

'I'll go and finish washing up.' Nona took herself off discreetly, shooting an amused look Janet's way.

They entered the bare, cheerless room, devoid now of all personal possessions, the dim lights casting ghostly glows over the ugly old-fashioned furniture.

Pushing the door to behind him, Bruce drew Janet into his arms. They embraced long and ardently. 'This week has been like a year to me,' he said gruffly, his lips against her throat.

'It's been like ten to me,' she choked, half laughingly, resting her head against him. She looked up into his blue eyes and scolded lightly, 'Why didn't you tell me about the track?'

'You weren't exactly in a listening mood, if you remember,' he said drily. 'I flew to Madrid as soon as I heard because I knew you'd never manage the legal side yourself. I planned to tell you on my return that I'd bought it in your mother's name,' he sloped his smile, 'but my little surprise backfired.'

'I deserve all I've suffered this week,' Janet admitted penitently. She asked after a moment, 'Is it true what Mother said, that you own the villa?'

Bruce nodded. 'The Westons are old friends of mine. They were anxious to be rid of all their overseas property, so I took the villa off their hands. I bought it solely for investment purposes. Then the Fords wrote and complained that they were having trouble parking their cars, so I flew out to see what the problem was.' He gave Janet his blue gleam. 'I was determined to have the track for the villa, but you kept getting in the way of my intentions.'

'I noticed you kept me at a distance.' She slanted him a sideways smile.

'I tried to.' He gripped her. 'But I not only ended up becoming more and more settled in Ibiza, I was also in danger of losing my head over an important legal matter. I decided the only thing to do was to marry you to keep my sanity and my profession.'

'And of course that way you get to keep the track in the family too,' she teased. 'The villa being right next door.'

His gaze lapsed whimsical. 'I don't see us doing much entertaining,' he said vibrantly against her throat. 'What friends we have can come in at the front.'

'Are we really going to live there?' Janet asked dreamily.

'That's how I planned it,' Bruce nodded. 'I've arranged to practise permanently in Spain, covering Ibiza and the mainland. Francisco is handling the Madrid office. He likes city life.'

Janet tilted him a look. 'I remember he used to like beach life too,' she twinkled accusingly, 'until you put a stop to our little jaunts.'

'I admit it,' he said gruffly, dropping his face into her hair. 'I've never been able to bear seeing you with another man.' As though to reassure himself that she really was his, he searched out her lips again.

After a long moment she drew away and said shyly,

noticing his loose raincoat for the first time, 'You're all wet.'

He nodded. 'I took a bus and walked the rest of the way.' He glanced around the cheerless candle-lit room and said in dry tones, 'Not exactly home from home, is it?'

'We're just leaving.' Janet explained. 'Nona is married now. She was going to put me up at her place for a while.'

'I have no intention of letting you out of my sight again,' he glinted down at her, smiling. 'My club is just a bus ride away. There's a hotel opposite. We'll put you up there for tonight and fly out tomorrow. That's if you fancy getting married in Ibiza?'

Janet tilted her head and met his gaze. 'I think Mother would like that,' she said with a humorous twinkle.

'I think she would,' he replied with an equally humorous gleam. He turned an arm about her waist and asked deeply, 'You won't mind if our children grow up into country urchins, speaking Spanish as well as English?'

'How could I mind anything as wonderful as that?' she laughed, the pink in her cheeks enhancing the stars in her eyes.

There was a loud knock on the door. Nona pushed her way in and quipped, 'I'm sorry to have to butt in on you two, but I have to go now. The kitchen's all finished and Robbie's waiting.'

With Bruce alongside her Janet moved out into the gloom of the hallway. The front door was open. She followed Nona's gaze out to where a van was running gently on its engine in the light of the street lamp. She smiled humbly, 'I won't be going with you now.'

'That doesn't surprise me,' Nona quirked, as she slipped on her coat. She hugged Janet and said with a bantering smile, 'Write me a letter some time.'

'Oh, I will!' Janet replied with a starry gaze.

'I've blown the candles out in the kitchen,' her friend said, stepping outside around the luggage and packages in the hall.

'Don't worry about these, Nona,' Bruce said, smiling. 'We'll come back and pick them up in the morning.'

While she was going down the steps, Janet went to blow out the last of the candles. She had only to slip off her work overall and put on her coat. With everything packed and the place in complete darkness she would have to manage as she was for one night.

Nona had arrived at the van when she got back to the door. She saw Robert start to get out. He couldn't understand why his wife was ushering him back. There were several moments of whispered confusion inside the cab, then Nona waved. The van started to move slowly away from the curb. Before he took it off with a loud roar of the engine Robert waved too. Soon there was nothing to be seen but the red light receding in the distance.

Bruce buttoned up his coat against the squally night. 'Ready?' he asked quizzically as Janet stepped out with him. Nodding, she changed the key in the door and locking up she dropped the keys into her handbag. They walked down the steps hand in hand. The wind gusted along the street behind them. Droplets scattered across the glistening pavements.

Janet knew no discomfort walking through the rainswept night. With Bruce's arm around her she was oblivious to everything but an all-consuming happiness.

EACH MONTH —
FOUR GREAT NOVELS

Here are the Latest Titles:

PLEASE NOTE: All Harlequin Presents novels from #83 onwards are 95c. Books below that number, **where available** are priced at 75c through Harlequin Reader Service until December 31st, 1975.

These titles are available at your local bookseller, or through the Harlequin Reader Service, M.P.O. Box 707, Niagara Falls, N.Y. 14302; Canadian address 649 Ontario St., Stratford, Ont.